W9-CFR-102

She wanted the moment to last forever...

It wasn't fair, Julie thought, that such a wonderful moment of enlightenment should be so brief. Evidently Felipe did not share her own feelings of joy at the discovery of her love for him.

Instead he spoke about Majorca, and she asked, "Have you always lived on the island?"

"No," he said, "the family home is in Cadiz. I spent my holidays here with my grandparents."

"How nice that a place as beautiful as this should hold such happy memories for you," she remarked, envying the island because it had known him far longer than she had.

"I trust the island will hold happy memories for you, also," Felipe replied softly.

And Julie wondered whether she would have happiness to remember — or tragedy.

KATRINA BRITT
is also the author of these
Harlequin Romances

and this
Harlequin Presents

Many of these titles are available at your local bookseller.

For a free catalogue listing all available Harlequin Romances
and Harlequin Presents, send your name and address to:

HARLEQUIN READER SERVICE
1440 South Priest Drive, Tempe, AZ 85281
Canadian address: Stratford, Ontario N5A 6W2

Hotel Jacarandas

by

KATRINA BRITT

Harlequin Books

TORONTO • LONDON • LOS ANGELES • AMSTERDAM
SYDNEY • HAMBURG • PARIS • STOCKHOLM • ATHENS • TOKYO

Original hardcover edition published in 1980
by Mills & Boon Limited

ISBN 0-373-02449-5

Harlequin edition published January 1982

Copyright © 1980 by Katrina Britt.
Philippine copyright 1980. Australian copyright 1980.

All rights reserved. Except for use in any review, the reproduction or utilization
of this work in whole or in part in any form by any electronic, mechanical or
other means, now known or hereafter invented, including xerography,
photocopying and recording, or in any information storage or retrieval system,
is forbidden without the permission of the publisher, Harlequin Enterprises
Limited, 225 Duncan Mill Road, Don Mills, Ontario, Canada M3B 3K9. All the
characters in this book have no existence outside the imagination of the
author and have no relation whatsoever to anyone bearing the same name
or names. They are not even distantly inspired by any individual known
or unknown to the author, and all the incidents are pure invention.

The Harlequin trademark, consisting of the words HARLEQUIN ROMANCE
and the portrayal of a Harlequin, is registered in the United States Patent
Office and in the Canada Trade Marks Office.

Printed in U.S.A.

CHAPTER ONE

'GUESS what?' exclaimed Julie across the breakfast table. 'Daddy has invited me to spend my holiday with him in Majorca!'

She looked up from the letter in her hand to meet the soft blue gaze of her mother looking bandbox fresh in her business suit of lavender blue. How young she looks, Julie thought tenderly, not a day over thirty-five, with her golden hair neatly coiffed around her small head and her English rose complexion. How her father could have left her for a girl half her age was beyond her.

Her father's job as an international banker had taken him abroad frequently and her mother, tired of being a grass widow, had taken a job as chief buyer for a famous London fashion house. Her work had often taken her abroad too, with the result that they had rarely been home at the same time.

The break finally came when her father had resigned from his job in favour of hotel management and had gone to keep a hotel in Majorca, taking with him a girl who had been Julie's best friend, Dale Francis.

They had worked at the same bank, and Julie recalled with regret the times she had brought Dale home for company when her mother had been away. On several of these occasions her father had taken them both out to dinner, and Dale had made no secret of her admiration for him, although he was much older, forty-eight to Dale's twenty-four.

Her mother said quietly, 'I'm glad. You will go, of course? More coffee?'

Julie noticed the colour creep up under her clear skin as it was wont to do whenever her father was mentioned. Her mother's hand holding the coffee percolator was trembling slightly as well, and Julie wondered how much she missed her husband. She missed her father dreadfully herself.

She waved the coffee away, having lost the taste for it.

'No, thanks,' she answered. 'Sure you don't mind if I go to see Daddy? We had planned to spend our holiday together, remember?'

Her mother's smile was sweet. 'There'll be other times. You'll enjoy it.'

'But what about Dale? Won't it be embarrassing for her?'

Her mother lifted slender shoulders. 'Dale can cope.'

She was right, Julie thought. A girl who could run away with a married man could cope with anything. She perused the letter again, seeing it as a beckoning finger luring her on to the beautiful sun-kissed isle off the Cala d'Oro.

Dreamily she pictured shallow, sandy coves caressed by a warm azure sea where one could recline beneath the shelter of a sunshade and sample the thirst-quenching delight of ice-cool melon.

Her mother broke into her thoughts with amusement.

'I wish you could see your face! It's a picture of utter bliss. Darling, it's what the doctor ordered. You've never fully recovered from that bad attack of 'flu last year.'

For the first time in ages Julie found herself avoiding the tender blue gaze, for they both knew that it had been more than an attack of 'flu. It had been the time when her father had left home for good, and it had broken Julie's heart.

Her love for her father had turned to hate at first until she began to realise that it had not been entirely his fault. She remembered all the heavenly times they had enjoyed together as a family, the times when he had taken her out to dinner because her mother happened to be away travelling for her firm. Then gradually her hate turned into pity because her father would never be happy with Dale—not after knowing Mummy. Of this Julie was sure.

Now she was on her way to see him again, and a lump rose in her throat as the plane zoomed towards majestic brown peaks, snow-breasted and outlined against the eye-watering blue of the sky. White crevasses meandered down from the snowy tips to cascade over ledges on their way down the luscious greenness of the lower slopes.

Julie caught her breath at the awe-inspiring sight of something bigger than mere mortals as more peaks came into view ahead of the wing-tip of the plane which seemed to be standing still in silent homage.

'Wonderful view,' chirped the elderly woman sitting next to Julie. 'Kind of sobers you and makes you want to cry. I adore the Pyrenees.'

Julie smiled in agreement and nodded, having no desire to talk just then. She was recalling how she had pleaded with her father not to go away, saying it was enough just for them to be together. But he had gone, and she had cried herself to sleep at night sick with the sense of loss, anger, and misery.

In the tiny washroom of the plane, Julie scanned her face anxiously in the mirror. She had inherited her mother's clear skin, but her hair was tawny and apt to fall in thick heavy natural waves, whereas her mother's hair was gold and finer. She had her father's deep brown eyes and thick lashes and her mother's delicate nose. Her mouth, like her father's, had a habit of turning up at the corners in a ready smile like his.

Julie used her lipstick and combed out her tawny locks and returned to her seat to fasten her seat belt for landing. Here I go, she thought. I hope Daddy hasn't changed in any way, especially towards me.

On leaving the Customs, Julie was looking for a taxi when the long black shiny limousine drew up silently beside her, and a tall man extricated himself from behind the wheel, faultlessly attired in a light-weight suit of impeccable cut. She had the impression of well developed shoulders, well groomed tobacco brown hair covering a well-shaped head, and the most breathtaking dark eyes looking down into hers.

She recovered her breath to put him in the late twenties age group as he had a look of experience combined with a hint of arrogance which was by no means off-putting. On the contrary, his smile was wholly charming even if it was just slightly aloof.

'Miss Julie Denver?' he queried in a rich deep brown voice in slightly accented English.

'Yes,' she replied on breath regained.

He smiled and the flash of white teeth lightened the dark arrogantly cut features.

'You will permit me to escort you to the hotel Jacarandas. You will please sit in the car while I attend to your case.'

As he opened the car door for her to slide into the spacious leather interior, she noticed the intricately carved antique ring on the third finger of his right hand.

The car was well on its way when she ventured to speak hoping to keep the anxiety of her thoughts from her voice. For some reason or other the gorgeous man sitting silently beside her gave the impression that he would view any show of emotion with a certain amount of distaste.

'My father? He is well?' she asked tentatively.

'Your father is perfectly well, Miss Denver. At the moment he is exceedingly busy with every room booked for the season, and as I was coming this way I offered to pick you up.'

'That was very kind of you,' she answered with relief, and her mouth curved in a tender smile. 'I'm glad he's successful.'

'Did you doubt that he would not succeed in his venture?'

His tones were a trifle sharp and Julie stole a glance at that clear-cut profile that would have graced a rare coin.

'Not really. Daddy can make a success of anything he undertakes. He caused quite a stir when he left the banking world, but this is something he's always wanted to do.'

'Your father brought a wealth of experience into his present venture. He had travelled all over the world and his knowledge of hotels has been an important factor in his success. He has a brilliant lively mind and I am proud to have him as a friend.'

She said carefully, 'Are you in the hotel business?'

He tossed her a swift glance of unsmiling consideration.

'I happen to own the Hotel Jacarandas.'

'You own hotels?'

'No. The hotel happens to be one of my ancestral homes,' he informed her laconically.

He said no more and Julie changed the conversation, for the journey was not without interest. The road they were taking wound its way through fields dotted by windmills used for irrigation.

'Is this the Cala d'Oro road?' she enquired politely.

'It is. We have only one main motorway.'

Julie glanced swiftly at the brown well kept hands on the car wheel. They looked strong and dependable, like the man himself.

'Is it far to the hotel?' she asked.

'About half an hour by car, which is one of the reasons why it is so popular, situated as it is away from the bustling capital. Soon we shall be passing through Manacor, famous for its furniture and manufactured pearls.'

Julie looked out eagerly at the passing landscape as he put on speed, and emitted exclamations of surprise and pleasure. The sun was seeping its warmth into her very bones and the feeling was one of utter bliss.

'Almond trees,' he murmured, seeing her give rapt attention to regiments of trees in an orchard. 'The almond harvest is very interesting. The farmers use very long poles to gather in the almonds, standing on carpets of green sheets spread beneath the trees.'

He gave her some of the history of the island and his easy flow of words did much to relax her tension until her incipient unease melted away. Julie fixed her gaze on the distant hills behind which lay she knew not what. What would her arrival hold for her? Would Dale be resentful—as Julie could hardly see her being party to the invitation her father had sent? One thing about her father was that he was not easily led. He could be as stubborn as her mother. But stubborness, Julie thought sadly, could be as dangerous as weakness.

The car dipping into an incline in the road gave them an exciting glimpse of golden beaches through the trees. Then the glimpse widened into a picture-postcard view of blue, blue sea enriched by sweeping vistas of the kind of beaches one dreams of in English winter. And there perched high above it stood the Hotel

Jacarandas, built into a rocky cove.

Julie's gaze wandered over the sun-soaked paradise through brilliant flower-filled gardens and tree-shaded terraces down, down to the sand below.

The Hotel Jacarandas, with blue shutters, was surrounded by tall pines. There was a long verandah running along the length of the upper floors, part of which was covered by gaily striped sunshades. Julie smiled up at her companion. Her eyes danced as soon her sandalled feet would on the the sun-warmed earth.

'It's beautiful!' she gasped.

The dark eyes turned her way, lingering so long on her animated face that she almost asked if she had dirt on her nose. His slow smile when it came was utterly disarming.

'I am pleased that you like it,' he said.

The next moment he was out of the car and taking her case from the trunk. Julie paused inside the entrance, blinking a little bemusedly after the eye-watering light outdoors. The marble floor of the foyer gleamed with a richness one accredited to the entrance of a palace. Muted light came from a wall of windows where delicate frilly curtains shrouded the glare of the sun. They were transparent and sparklingly fresh in their neatness. Julie had little time to take in the elegance of furniture and flower arrangements on tables and in alcoves for a man came hurrying to greet them as they entered.

Julie's companion spoke in crisp tones and surrendered her case.

'Ah, Tomas, show Señorita Denver to her room,' he said crisply. Then turning to Julie he politely bade her *adios*.

Julie liked the young man confronting her. Short and round, he had an infectious smile and there was no mistaking his appraisal of her in his dark eyes.

'*Buenas tardes*, Señorita Denver. Welcome to the Hotel Jacarandas. Do you speak Spanish at all?'

Julie shook her bright head. 'Not very well, I'm afraid. I have the usual small phrase-book which I hope will get me by.'

'You will learn as you go along,' he assured her. 'I will be delighted to help you at any time.' He gave her a courteous small bow. 'Tomas Venegas at your service.'

She thanked him, but she was on pins to meet her father, and suddenly there he was striding across the foyer to meet her with such a wealth of love in his eyes as to bring tears to her own.

'Daddy!' she cried, and flung herself into his arms.

As they hugged and kissed Julie noticed that he was deeply tanned, and at first glance he did not appear to have changed at all. But a second glance showed a kind of strained look. He looked tired and lean ... too lean.

'How are you ... and Dale?' she asked, smiling up at him mistily.

'We're both fine. You don't put on any weight,' he teased.

'Neither do you,' she replied, feeling choked. 'It's sweet of you to ask me to come.'

'How's your mother?' he asked.

'As lovely as ever. I have two beautiful parents and I'm in love with both of you. I'll always love you both dearly.'

Her father kissed the top of her tawny head quickly and placed an arm around her shoulders.

'I'll take you to your room,' he said. 'Tomas will have already taken your case. How long can you stay?'

'Three weeks.'

The upper floors of the hotel were reached by lifts and a beautifully waxed oak staircase. Throughout the entire building huge crystal chandeliers glittered down on superbly tiled floors and velvet piled Wilton carpet.

Her room on the second floor had its own bath, shower and bidet. The carpet was off-white and the deep rose colour of the bedspread echoed in the cushions and lampshades.

'It's lovely.' Julie gazed around the room with shining eyes and hugged her father.

'I want you to have a good holiday,' he said soberly. 'I've been looking forward to you coming. Sorry I couldn't meet you at the airport. What do you think of the Señor?'

Julie tossed her shoulder bag on to the bed, having forgotten her escort from the airport. The excitement of arriving and seeing her father again had driven the encounter temporarily from her mind. She had dismissed it as being impersonal to the extreme. Now upon reflection she again felt the tingling sensation evoked by dark exciting features, a slow charming smile and deep cultured voice.

She laughed. 'I don't even know what his name is.'

'Felipe de Torres y Aquiliño. He has other christian names, but he's always called Don Felipe. His family owned most of the island at one time and this hotel is part of his estate. Like everyone else he's been hit by inflation and now runs a farm to the north of the island. He has a valuable herd of cattle, vineyards and a well run farm comprising almond and fruit orchards as well as other interests. He's also a splendid horseman and keeps a good stable of thoroughbreds.'

'A Spaniard in boots,' Julie laughed. 'I bet they're as highly polished as the man himself.'

'I like him. But he doesn't approve of divorce. He says I took a gamble which didn't pay off.'

Julie latched on quickly. 'A gamble, Daddy? Did you take a gamble? With Mummy?'

He seemed about to say something, then shrugged weary shoulders. 'If I did it's all in the past, so let it ride.'

She said resignedly, 'I suppose you're right.' Then because she had to know she added, 'Are you happy, Daddy?'

'If you can measure happiness by achieving an ambition, I suppose I am.'

Julie walked up to him and hugged him. 'You don't sound very convincing,' she said against his chest.

He kissed her hair. 'I'm very happy now that you are here. Will that do?'

'Am I intruding?'

Dale's voice struck Julie's ears like a gong and she moved away from her father to see her standing in the doorway regarding them warily. Her oval face had been too sallow for beauty, but she had changed. The Spanish sun had given her skin the ripe bloom of a peach. The dark brown hair which she wore long, loose and parted down the centre had golden lights in it and there was a radiance about her that reminded Julie of a girl in love.

Who had wrought the miracle? Was it her father? If it was someone else, Julie hoped with a pang that her father would not get hurt.

She smiled. 'Hello, Dale. I hardly recognised you, you look so well. How are you?'

'I'm fine. How are you?'

Dale's grey eyes were wary as she came forward with a slight smile. She was wearing riding clothes with a smart tailored sleeveless blouse.

Julie murmured that she was fine too, adding lightly, 'So you've taken up riding again?'

Dale moved over to the dressing table mirror and smoothed down her hair before moving in closer to examine a tiny blemish on her chin.

'Yes, I have,' she answered without turning round. 'There are excellent riding stables here. You must come riding with me. How long are you staying?'

'Three weeks,' Julie answered, wondering if she could stand it if the present atmosphere was anything to go by. 'I've lots of news from the bank. Flavia is married and Richard is engaged.'

Dale swung round and Julie saw the colour rush beneath the golden tan. Richard Telfor, a blond Don Juan, had been her favourite date until he had ditched her for someone else—Flavia.

Julie went on lightly, 'Richard's fiancée is French. Flavia has married a wealthy industrialist.'

'Surprise, surprise!' Dale laughed on regained breath. 'Maybe I ought to have hung around a little longer. I've ordered tea in our sitting room, the last door along the corridor to the right. Give me time to change, then we can have a natter. See you!'

It was then Julie noticed that her father had left the room. When Dale had gone she stood for a while wondering what the situation was between them. Presently, leaving her unpacking until later, she took a shower and slipped on a crisp cool cotton frock suitable for the occasion. She spread her modest toilet things on the glass-topped dressing table, combed her hair and made up her face lightly.

By now the thought of a cup of tea was more than welcome, and Julie hoped her father would be there with Dale. She worried about him and hoped that he was happy.

Her paternal grandmother had taken her son's divorce philosophically. 'Richard has made his bed and now he must lie in it,' she had said firmly.

Julie had agreed, but like her grandmother she had taken it to heart. She had learned that when one truly loves someone one goes on loving them no matter what they do.

The room she entered was spacious, the furnishings —a mixture of antique and modern—blended by a master hand. The tall windows framed panoramic views of the sea and gardens and Julie strolled over to them.

A covered tray had been set down on a small table on the shady verandah and the scent of vine leaves impregnated by blossom stole over her senses like a caress.

Dale came in wearing a demure little dress which she explained immediately.

'I help out on reception. Sit down and tell me all the news.'

Julie obliged and found it easy going with Dale eager for gossip. Later, Julie discovered that her father had his office along the same corridor, and she went along to see him in lighthearted mood.

She found his door slightly ajar and peeped in to see him gazing through the window enjoying a cigarette.

'Hi!' she cried. 'Want any help?'

It was a small room dominated by a huge desk filled with papers. There was a filing cabinet and two comfortable chairs and the place looked very masculine. Julie noticed a door leading to another room.

'Hello there.' Her father turned and gave her a fond smile. 'You're here for a holiday, my pet. I want you to enjoy yourself.'

'I shall,' she assured him with confidence. Since her chat with Dale Julie's spirits had soared. 'I thought you'd given up smoking, Daddy?'

His smile was rueful. 'I did. I hope you don't follow my example.'

She laughed. 'I'm going to buy a few cards to send home. I must write to Gran to tell her how you are, but I won't mention the smoking. She always said you smoked too much. Can I bring you anything from the shops?'

He turned to stub out his cigarette on an ashtray on the table.

'No, thanks. You can get your cards from our shop downstairs in the foyer. How is Gran?'

Julie sobered. 'She misses you—we all do. See you later.'

She bought a series of coloured scenes of the island for Gran and her mother from the little shop in the hotel foyer and pictured Gran eagerly devouring her news in her lovely cottage near the Sussex Downs.

Later she went down to the village to post the cards and to browse around the shops. Among the fashion wear and leather goods were ideal presents to take home and she spent a pleasant hour or so filling the straw bag she had bought with her purchases.

The village was within easy walking distance from the hotel and she was about to make her way back when the big car slid up beside her.

'Permit me?'

The car door swung open and Don Felipe was smiling at her.

Julie taken aback hitched her shoulder bag and clutched her shopping bag.

'I ... I was about to walk back to the hotel,' she stammered. 'Are you going that way?'

He reached out to relieve her of the shopping bag by tossing it on to the back seat of the car, then leaned forward after she had sat down beside him to ensure that her door was fastened.

'It is far too warm for you to walk at this time of the day,' he said coolly by way of reply.

Julie looked up from fastening her seat belt to meet an expression in his eyes that could only be described as impersonal. Correct was hardly the word for it, she thought resentfully.

His manner, bordering on the cordial, was distinctly formal as he turned his head to start the car.

'It seems that I am for ever in your debt,' she began with a touch of lightness, her eyes on his clear-cut profile. 'I'd like to thank you for giving me the lift from the airport. If ... if there's anything I can do for you in exchange, I will. You're very kind.'

She knew she was babbling, but the man had her on edge. He could not have affected her more had he made a pass at her. There was no explanation for the effect he had on her, since there was not even a hint of snobbery in his whole manner. Unfailingly courteous, he was just giving her a lift. Why make heavy weather of it?

Suddenly she was smiling. The sea and sky were so blue, and there was a quality of magic in the air.

He tossed her a glance. 'Do not be so casual in handing out your favours. I might take you up on that.'

Julie felt her face go hot. 'What else can I say to a man who appears to have everything?' she exclaimed.

'Everything?' He savoured the word with a frown. 'There are many things I do not possess.'

She said rather stiffly, 'I meant material things. I can hardly give you anything else.' She hurried on to cover her confusion. Was he deliberately trying to embarrass her?

'Are you married, Don Felipe?'

The words were out before she could prevent them. She could easily have asked her father, she thought with dismay. It just went to show how bemused she was in this man's company.

'No,' he answered after a pause. 'Is this your first visit to Majorca, Miss Denver?'

'Yes,' she replied, thinking that he did not intend to disclose anything about himself. He had no intention of improving upon their relationship despite two encounters. He was giving her a lift, that was all.

They arrived back at the hotel before either of them could continue the conversation and he dropped her off at the entrance.

'*Muchas gracias*, Don Felipe,' she said.

'*Adios*, Miss Denver,' he replied, and was gone.

CHAPTER TWO

JULIE slept well that night, and awoke to a day of warmth and sunshine. Birds were singing in the eaves as she padded to the window to see a sky of eye-watering blue. It was going to be a wonderful holiday. The important thing was not to think of Daddy in terms of Mummy. It was going to be a bit tricky, but she would manage it.

A maid came bearing a covered tray that smelled of freshly baked bread and coffee. There was butter, honey, a bunch of grapes and a slice of melon.

Julie smiled. '*Muchas gracias*,' she said. 'I could have come down to the dining room.'

The girl was pure Spanish, so it came as a surprise to hear her speak perfect English.

'It's a pleasure, miss,' she replied in very good English.

'You speak very good English,' Julie exclaimed. 'You look so Spanish.'

'I am Spanish—I work at the hotel to learn English. I am eighteen. I can write English much better than I can speak it.'

'You're doing extremely well,' said Julie, admiring the lovely olive-skinned, oval face in a frame of glossy jet black hair. The girl was sturdily built and Julie added, 'Are you a country girl from a farm—*finca*? I ask because you have such a lovely complexion, as if you'd been reared on peaches and grapes.'

The girl laughed, showing white teeth, and touched her face delightedly.

'*Muchas gracias*,' she smiled. 'I must tell my *novio*

that his Lucia has been fed on peaches and grapes.'

'You are engaged?'

'I am engaged to Tomas who works here.'

Julie recalled Tomas meeting her in the foyer and decided that they would make an ideal couple.

Lucia said, 'If there is anything else you may require, miss, you have only to ring the bell by your head. I will attend to your laundry or any pressing of your clothes.'

Julie was finishing her breakfast when Dale walked in. She looked very attractive in a sun-dress of glazed cotton. Julie liked the design of poppies on a white background and her high-heeled sandals.

Dale said, 'I wonder if you'd care to come with me. I'm going sick visiting, an elderly lady who lives in the village. She's the aunt of a friend of mine.'

Julie warmed to her friendly overture. What qualms she had about Dale's attitude towards her were fast disappearing.

'I'd love to,' she replied.

They went in Dale's small car. There was only a handful of houses among the restaurants and chic boulevard cafés in the small town. Some of them had been renovated and were smart with paint and colourful flower boxes. A few were neglected, the stucco of their façades discoloured and peeling.

Dale parked the car in a narrow cobbled street, then led the way to a rather large house that had mellowed through the years. An elderly woman in black admitted them into the cool dim interior and led the way up a beautifully carved staircase to the second floor.

The room they entered was spacious but sombre with heavy furniture. Bars of sunlight struck across the room from the covered windows to alight on the big beautifully carved bed and Dale moved across the room towards it with flowers and a basket of goods.

The lady sitting propped up with pillows looked

frail beneath the lace mantilla, but the dark eyes were very much alive in her small face. She greeted Dale affectionately as she received her kiss on her parchment-like cheek and smiled at Julie with a friendly warmth.

Dale said, 'Señora la Guardia, may I present Miss Julie Denver, the daughter of Mr Denver by a previous marriage. Julie, Doña Conchita.'

Julie tried not to wince at the 'previous marriage' bit and greeted the lady cordially. Dale had brought a basket of fruit, a chicken, chicken broth and a cake.

Doña Conchita spoke English remarkably well and enquired about London, of which she was fond. They spent a pleasant hour chatting and drinking chocolate, and were leaving the house when they collided with a young man who was about to enter.

He wore riding clothes and Julie was aware of black eyes staring at her curiously.

Dale said brightly, 'Julie, this is José la Guardia, Doña Conchita's nephew. José, I'm sure you'll be delighted to meet Julie Denver—I told you she was coming to stay with us for a holiday.'

He gave Julie the briefest of bows, greeting her in Spanish and, adding a few hurried words to Dale, went into the house.

Dale said as they entered the car, 'José and I always use Spanish when we meet. He's teaching me.'

Recalling the intimate look that had passed between them Julie wondered what else José could have been teaching Dale. Was it her imagination, the sudden shining of Dale's eyes, the extra lightness in her step? The next moment Julie was reprimanding herself for being unnaturally suspicious when she had always prided herself on being neither bitchy nor malicious.

They had a delightful lunch in the village with Dale being her old self. She could be nice when she chose. Sitting beneath the colourful awning, Julie looked

around for her knight errant, Don Felipe. A tingle of
excitement ran through her at the thought of meeting
him again. No use telling herself that she was foolish
to think about a man who had given her a lift twice in
his car, who with a casual wave of a long brown hand
had gone without any further thoughts of one Julie
Denver.

He interested her greatly even though somehow she
felt that she would never really know this man of the
beautiful voice, searching dark eyes and charming
smile, all of which enchanted her.

During lunch Dale mentioned a local beautician who
had a high-class establishment over a dress shop.

'Do come with me,' she begged. 'Arturo does wonders
with my skin. I go for a facial once a week if I can
spare the time, and it's a must against the sun. He uses
all kind of oils and things and I come away feeling like
a million pounds.'

Julie laughed. 'I didn't know money had feelings.
I've never had a facial, but I'll take your word for it.'

The salon was the last word in luxury, with prices
to match. The decor was white and deep mauve and the
assistants moved around like dancers in lilac pink
overalls. Arturo had the most beautiful hands Julie
had seen, long tapering fingers, strong yet gentle, that
moved over the skin like a cool breeze. There were cold
compresses and hot ones, oils and creams, all applied to
a background of muted music.

He complimented Julie on her luxuriant tawny hair
which he styled lovingly into its natural way of growth.
Her face glowed from the delicate massage.

'Not bad, Dale, not bad at all. I really do feel like a
million,' she said as they left the shop.

They were laughing when the big car slid by, its
driver lifting a hand in salute. Julie was aware of the
white gleam of teeth in a brown disturbing face and the

instant recognition of dark eyes.

They waved back and she said rather breathlessly, 'Don Felipe—he's rather attractive, isn't he?'

Dale shrugged but did not answer. They were back in the car when Julie said curiously, 'Don't you care for our handsome Spaniard.'

'Let's say there's no love lost on both sides.'

Dale drove along the narrow street and looked both ways before driving out into the main road.

Julie wrinkled her youthful brow. 'I'm sure you're wrong. Don Felipe has confessed a liking for Daddy.'

Dale said philosophically, 'I suppose it's because they're both well educated men with a lot in common. Felipe spent some years in England at university. I know Ricky likes him.'

Julie swallowed. Dale referring to her own father as Ricky stuck in her throat. Her mother had always called him Rick, a shortened version of Richard. Ricky sounded too young, too naïve for Daddy, but she was glad that Dale did not use her mother's pet name for him. To Julie's way of thinking it put her mother on another plane from Dale.

Julie smiled as her father greeted them in the foyer of the hotel on their return. His eyes flitted appraisingly from one young glowing face to the other.

'What have you been doing to yourselves?' he teased. 'You look blooming, like two delicious peaches ripening in the sun. Enjoy your day out?'

'Very much,' Julie answered. 'What kind of a day have you had?'

'Not bad,' he volunteered. He looked at Dale. 'Come on, you're late for reception.'

Dale positively bristled as she glared at him. 'I know. Don't push me around!'

He said quietly, 'I never push you around—you

know that. I only expect you to consider the staff as they consider you.'

Dale made no reply. She tossed her head and stalked to the reception desk. Julie felt her father's arm around her shoulders as they crossed the foyer to the lift.

She said tentatively, 'Does Dale have to work on reception? Are you hard up or something?'

They were in the lift when he replied. 'It's a case of giving her something to do. She'll only be on duty for two hours to relieve the staff. I happen to be a little on the old-fashioned side in believing that the devil finds work for idle hands to do.'

Julie swallowed on a mound of remembered pain.

'You're a little late to philosophise, aren't you, Daddy?' she reminded him bitterly. 'You left Mummy alone for weeks on end when you worked for the bank —or weren't you so concerned about what she did when you were away?'

Her father went strangely white beneath his tan and it occurred to Julie that he looked very tired. He said sternly,

'We won't mention your mother again while you're here, Julie. You understand?'

She felt suddenly ashamed. I've hurt him, she thought, and I would never do that willingly.

'I'm sorry, Daddy.' She was very contrite. 'It was wrong of me to interfere in something I don't understand. I love you too much to hurt you. I do apologise.'

She hugged his arm as they left the lift and rubbed her head against him. He patted her hand on his arm.

'Don't be too upset about it,' he whispered gently. 'I have news for you. Don Felipe is giving a party here at the hotel this evening for some American guests he has staying at his farm, and we've been invited. He wants it to be a Spanish-style evening with all the traditional dancing and singing. We have an excellent dance floor here and a superb cabaret, both of which are the reason for Don Felipe coming here.

Julie was glad about her facial and hair-styling of that morning as she prepared for the evening's entertainment. They had given her a kind of glow—or was it the fact that she was going to see Don Felipe again?

The black velvet evening top and flowered silk panne velvet skirt looked a little Spanish, and she found herself wishing idiotically that she had the traditional smouldering black eyes and dark hair as silky as a raven's wing. Would she look insipid against the glowing beauty of Don Felipe's womenfolk?

Dale joined her on the way downstairs looking dramatic in red, and her father followed in evening dress which he always wore so well.

There was a private room available for parties next to the restaurant in the hotel, and Julie felt her heartbeats quicken at the sight of Don Felipe there welcoming his guests.

He greeted them charmingly, sharing that white smile between them before giving his attention to other guests behind them.

Everyone drifted to the bar at the far end of the room and Julie was surprised to see José, Doña Conchita's nephew, there. He looked different in evening dress, almost good-looking, as his usual scowl was less in evidence.

Somehow Dale was by his side and they moved slightly away.

'What do you think of José, Daddy?' Julie asked under cover of the conversation around them as they sipped their drinks.

Her father shrugged. 'José is like a number of young people today who don't know what they want. He's

Doña Conchita's heir, which is quite something since she possesses very good jewellery and other assets. She's a distant relation of Felipe.'

Julie glanced uneasily at Dale and José, who were talking earnestly together. Her father had either not noticed them or was ignoring their existence.

She said curiously, 'Why is Don Felipe bringing his guests to the hotel to be entertained when he might easily entertain them at his home?'

Her father took down part of his drink. 'We happen to have some first class Spanish singers and dancers here at the hotel for the season and their contract doesn't allow for them entertaining elsewhere. Felipe has some American guests staying with him and he wants to give them a Spanish night out. That's why they're here.'

Julie watched Felipe moving about among his guests seeing that everyone had a drink, then pausing to talk to an American couple with a teenage son and daughter. The girl was smiling up at Felipe, who was bending his head to say something to her.

Julie felt a sudden urge to go to him to touch his immaculate arm, to tell him that she was here, jealous of the people who demanded his attention.

To her father, she said, 'Have you met Don Felipe's American guests?'

Her father finished his drink. 'They've been to the hotel for lunch several times.' He looked at his watch. 'I'm afraid I have to leave you for a while—I'm expecting some new arrivals. See you later. Have fun!'

'So soon, *amigo*?'

Julie's heart tilted, for Felipe was there, smiling. Glancing from one to the other, she could see the rapport between the two men. Both were tall with that natural ease of movement; her father with an air of good breeding instilled in him through the years;

Felipe fastidiously groomed in the manner of a Spanish grandee.

'Do you ride, Miss Denver?' Felipe was saying when her father had gone.

'A little, some years ago,' she admitted.

He smiled down at her and Julie had to lower her gaze. The surroundings, the laughter and chatter, the waiters bearing trays of drinks, the whole glittering evening might never have been. In that magical moment there was just Felipe and herself in the whole wide world.

Come, come, this won't do, Julie told herself sternly, realising how he was catching her interest. It was not just his looks and vibrant personality—she felt a kind of attraction that was impossible to ignore, but it was only on her side, and she was being idiotically naïve to take any notice of it.

She took a sip of her drink with a hand that was not quite steady and thought of the American girl who, moments before, had taken no pains to conceal her admiration for him. No reason why Julie Denver should repeat the performance.

'How do you like the island?' he asked.

'Very much. I adore the sun.'

He smiled, taking his time, looking at her hair and then her face growing hot beneath his scrutiny.

His voice was slightly mocking. 'An English rose blooming delightfully in the Spanish sun. What could be more enchanting?'

'A Spanish *señorita*, perhaps?'

He raised a dark silky brow and considered this. 'How does one define the beauty of a woman? By the tilt of her head, the flutter of delicate fingers, the delicate arch of her brows, the sweet cadence of her voice, her smile or the truth shining in her eyes?' Again his dark eyes were taking in the tawny hair. 'Her beautiful hair, perhaps, or the way her eyes tilt slightly at the corner like yours do in a way I find most intriguing.'

Julie had been drowning in the beauty of his deep voice and she found herself saying the first thing to come into her head.

'Daddy tells me you're giving your guests an evening of pure Spanish entertainment.'

'That is so. Come, I will introduce you to my American guests.'

He guided her across the room and Julie felt four pairs of eyes fixed curiously upon her as they approached the American family.

Stanley and Grace Main, with their daughter Sharon and son Roddy, greeted her cordially as Felipe introduced them. They chatted, had their drinks replenished and went in to dinner.

Julie found the meal as long-drawn-out as the interval before it and she did not really enjoy it. She lost count of the many courses as, seated between the American teenagers Sharon and Roddy Main, she could see Dale in deep conversation with her neighbour José la Guardia.

But it was Felipe of whom she was aware with every heart beat. In addition to the American couple his other guests were Spanish, mostly elderly and very correct. It was clear to Julie that everyone liked Felipe and the Americans were enchanted with him.

The entertainment which followed was excellent. It began with the single dramatic twang of a guitar leading the accompaniment in a slow stirring low beat that finally exploded into a crescendo. There was the clap of castanets, the rhythm quickened, rising to emotional heights, then plunged again into a pulsing whisper. The continual rise and fall of the music was enthralling. Julie was caught up with it, finding it as intoxicating as wine.

The group of dancers were terrific and the hours danced away with them. The finale held everyone spellbound as heels stumped, castanets clicked, and frilly skirts swirled with the dancers writhing madly to the music. The applause at the end was thunderous, and just before the lights went out over the dancers Julie saw her father standing at the far end of the room by the door.

When the lights came on she made her way across the room to him. She thought he looked tired, but decided against asking him if he was feeling all right.

'Enjoying it?' he asked with a smile.

'Very much. I think everyone did.' She looked anxiously at the tired lines around his eyes. It was frightening to see the humour gone from his face and he was looking years older.

'Did you have dinner?' she asked, trying to be casual.

He gave a mocking smile. 'Yes, I did.' He made a playful feint beneath her chin in the way he used to do when she was tiny. 'I hope Dale took care of you.'

'Yes, of course,' Julie assured him uneasily. 'Did you want her?'

'Not particularly.'

He was looking round the room and she followed his gaze. Waiters were moving around with trays of refreshments for the guests and she noticed Felipe having a word with a group of guitarists.

Her father was saying, 'There'll be songs now to round off the evening. See you later.'

Julie watched him go, then looked around once more for Dale. She was nowhere to be seen, neither was José. On an impulse she made for the garden and collided with Felipe.

His smile was mocking and just a little tight. 'You appear to be in a hurry, Miss Denver. It is not wise to rush out into the night air without a wrap.

Julie felt the blood rush to her face. She said hastily, 'I felt a need of fresh air. I don't intend to be out long enough to catch a chill.'

His hand was on her arm, setting all kinds of vibrations going inside her. He spoke quickly in an undertone. 'A word of advice. Do not interfere into what does not concern you.'

Julie froze and shook off his hand angrily.

'What's that supposed to mean?' she exclaimed and several of the guests strolling out into the gardens glanced curiously at them.

The next moment Felipe had her arm, this time in a vice like grip that marched her into the gardens. He did not release her until they were at the far end of the verandah out of earshot of other people.

His voice was as cold as the snows.

'Miss Denver.' A pause while he released her arm to lean back negligently against the frame of the tall windows to look down on her sternly. 'You have been invited to this island on a holiday. Let us leave it at that.'

Her skin prickled with indignation. How dared he meddle! She wanted to tell him to mind his own business, then decided to play it cool.

'I haven't the slightest idea what you're talking about. Will you please explain?' she said primly.

His mouth thinned. 'I have no intention of mentioning names since I do not discuss my friends behind their backs. I would advise you to do exactly what you came for and enjoy your holiday.'

Julie drew in a furious breath. 'Of all the nerve!' she cried, really incensed. 'You might be Daddy's

friend, but that doesn't give you the right to dictate
to me!'

Unperturbed, he said, 'I am a friend of your father's
and also a friend of yours. Please believe me when
I say that you will only make matters worse by interfering into what does not concern you. I have seen your
father looking much brighter for your coming. Do not
take that brightness away by actions which might prove
detrimental not only to him but to you also.'

She gave a small laugh which did not ring as true
as she would have liked.

'All this because I was going out for a breath of
fresh air! Why should you assume that I have some
ulterior motive for doing so?'

'I am no fool, Miss Denver. I usually manage to see
most things in their true perspective.' His voice had
slid on ice and her heart was just as cold. 'There are
some things in life that are best left to sort themselves
out, and I happen to think that this is one of them.
In any case, your interference will make things no
better.'

Julie bit hard on her lip. 'Thanks! You don't like
Dale, do you?'

A black silky eyebrow lifted provocatively. He said
stiffly,

'The question is irrelevant.'

'I know. You don't want to discuss it.'

He said in exasperation, 'For your own sake leave
well enough alone. Enjoy yourself while you are here.'

'How can I?' It was a cry from the heart. 'I love
my father. What kind of a person do you think I
am?'

'A sensible one. Do not forget that your father was
unhappy before he came here. He told me so.'

Julie backed against the stone balustrade of the verandah and placed her hands on the cold stone to pre-

vent them from trembling.

'You see things differently from the way we do. We're more enlightened regarding divorce,' she said thinly.

'I would hardly call it enlightened,' he said sardonically. 'We happen to have more reverence for our marriage vows, Miss Denver. Marriage is a contract which we give our word not to break until death us do part.'

She said tightly, 'Perhaps we marry for different reasons. We marry for love. My parents did. They were very happy before the divorce.'

'And you would call that true love, this feeling that failed the test of marriage?'

'Things happened that you wouldn't understand,' Julie protested. 'What did you mean when you said that Daddy took a gamble which failed?'

'I meant he gambled on your mother's love for him.'

'Did he tell you that?' She watched the dark inscrutable expression on his face and added wildly, 'Or did you guess it?'

He said coldly, 'Please keep your voice down. This is hardly the place for a discussion like this.'

'You began it, not I!'

'I refuse to argue with you. Your parents are a couple of blind idiots. In Spain a woman would not be allowed to get away with so much—they are content with being women and not hankering for men's shoes. You will be wise not to marry a man who is a man, one who is not to be trifled with.'

Her face went pale. 'By that I suppose you mean someone like you. Your advice is not needed. Like you, Don Felipe, I'm no fool.' She turned her back on him to grip the verandah with cold hands. 'Don't let me keep you from your guests.'

Time stood on a pinnacle of pain. She stood there

white and trembling. When she finally looked over her
shoulder, Felipe had gone.

The rest of the evening was like a dream. After the
traditional songs accompanied by the guitars, there
was dancing in which everyone joined in. Julie had no
lack of partners, but Felipe never came near.

She danced with Roddy Main, who told her that
he was nineteen and was studying law. He was a nice
boy to be with and when he asked her to go snorkelling with him the following day she accepted, seeing
it as a break from the hotel and from any embarrassing
meetings with Felipe.

CHAPTER THREE

NEVER before had Julie thought that a hotel could be such an enchanted place as the Jacarandas. Golden sunshine filled the grounds and the rooms with a mellowed radiance far too lovely for description. Sweet sounds filled the air, the trill of birds, laughter, or the lilt of a tune as a girl sang and a guitar twanged.

As she slipped on the sleeveless blue linen sun-dress over her brief swimsuit with snorkelling in mind, she was taking it for granted that Roddy was taking her snorkelling on his own. It was almost a shock therefore when the long limousine drew up at the hotel entrance on time to pick her up. Felipe unfolded his long length from the car, greeted her politely, then shut her in the back of the vehicle with Roddy while he slid in the front seat beside Sharon.

While Roddy, giving her a friendly smile, found he felt amazingly at ease with her. Normally he had been tonguetied with any girl, in spite of the fact that he had met plenty of them at home through his sister Sharon. But Julie was different, he thought exultantly. She was a real English rose with her exquisitely curved sensitive mouth, her air of tranquillity setting him at ease from the beginning.

With her he was able to lean back in his seat and relax without the necessity to make witty remarks or try to impress upon her his masculinity. This very pretty girl would understand if he was awkward in his speech. Watching her closely without appearing to do so, he noticed that there were shadows beneath the lovely eyes, and that her face was sad.

He wondered what was troubling her and felt suddenly very grown up and protective. During the drive Julie learned that Roddy, Sharon and Felipe were no strangers to snorkelling which left her the odd man out. On reaching the boat Sharon peeled off her clothing to reveal a bikini. Julie followed suit and felt less conspicious in a one-piece bathing suit.

While Sharon and Roddy put on their snorkelling gear, Felipe showed Julie how to put on hers. Showing her how to grip the rubber breathing tube between her teeth, he impressed upon her that this was her lifeline. His lean brown fingers worked confidently and soon he was giving her a last critical inspection. It was all a matter of course to him and he was about as genial as the snow-capped Pyrenees.

Things were the reverse with Julie as she tried to hide her nervousness at her initiation into the art of snorkelling. Felipe's presence should have given her a sense of security, but she did not find it very comfortable receiving favours from someone who obviously resented her and all she stood for.

They were all ready when Felipe dismissed Sharon and Roddy by saying that he proposed to take Julie down himself on her first venture into the deep.

He said gently, 'You have not lived until you go down beneath the waves to share the silent world with the creatures of the deep.' He patted her shoulder reassuringly before going over the side, leaving her standing for several seconds from sheer fright. Then pulling herself together, she slipped into the water.

After the initial shock of the depths of water Julie was conscious of a deep silence. She was aware of moving shadows as blues, greys and greens merged into a shimmering shoal of silver fish swimming by. There was a strange feeling in her ears, the water was heavy, yet swimming was easy.

Gripping the breathing pipe firmly between her teeth, she gazed in wonder through glass at a dream world of fantasy and beauty. An underwater garden of feathery fronds swaying to and fro as in a dance and flowers clinging to rocks was sheer poetry.

Then Felipe was there, closing in at the end of a stream of air bubbles to take her hand. Julie never forgot the next exciting interlude beneath the waves with him as her guide. His hand was warm and vibrant, sending a tingling through her veins. What if he was not for her nor she for him? At the moment he was part of the beauty around her.

All too soon they surfaced and Felipe was hauling her into the boat.

'Enjoy it?' he asked, helping her off with her gear.

'It was super!' she told him, looking up at him with shining eyes.

Drops of water cascaded down her face as he gave her a towel.

'You can go down again after lunch. No sense in overdoing it the first time,' he said.

Julie nodded, thankful to the roots that she had not made a fool of herself. Then Sharon and Roddy were clambering on board and Sharon was shedding her gear to stretch out in the sun, her golden brown body in the brief bikini looking like an advertisement in a glossy magazine.

They picnicked off delicate slices of succulent pork. Olives, black and inviting, were laid on crisp green leaves of lettuce, and there was fresh fruit washed down by iced wine.

Felipe was the charming host, concentrating his attention on Sharon, who thrived on his banter like a flower opening to the sun. Julie thought, he's only aloof and impersonal to me.

'How did you make out?' asked Roddy, sitting beside her.

'Fine,' she replied, and sighed, finding Roddy absurdly young compared with Felipe. She gazed at him tenderly as he ate his lunch in the manner of a small boy on an outing. Nevertheless, Roddy was on the threshold of being a man, with his somewhat stubborn jaw and the interested look in his eyes.

Her tender regard of Roddy was intercepted suddenly by Felipe's dark intent stare. She returned his look almost in bewilderment, as she had forgotten all about him in studying Roddy. Making a conscious effort and pushing all tension and unease away, she managed to produce a bright smile.

'*Muchas gracias* for the lunch, Don Felipe,' she said. 'I've enjoyed it immensely.'

He smiled, that charming smile that never failed to push her heart from its perch.

'*De nada*,' he replied. 'The pleasure is mine. It would give me greater pleasure if we were to dispense with formalities and you were to call me Felipe.'

'You must call me Julie,' she answered.

She was much more uneasy than she would have had him notice, for his glance and his words had shaken her. She could not make up her mind whether he was deliberately making her feel uncomfortable or amusing himself at her expense.

She was in another world where one breathed different air and the old set of values had been exchanged for unfamiliar ones—the leisurely way of living, the politeness at every turn, the sense of utter timelessness made it all seem like a dream.

After lunch they rested on deck, at least Sharon and Julie did. Felipe went down below to fetch up a map which he and Roddy studied.

Julie closed her eyes, thinking of Felipe and wishing

that his smile was not so terribly attractive. His deep voice conjured up a picture of what he was—lean, dark, and slightly sardonic, a cavalier in whose veins the blood of a long line of Spanish ancestors flowed.

When she opened her eyes again Felipe and Roddy were getting all the gear together for them to take a second plunge into the water.

Sharon said in an undertone to Julie, 'I suppose you're eager to go into the water again. I shall be going with Felipe.'

Julie wondered where this left her since she was there on Roddy's invitation and it was natural that she should pair off with him. It was a relief to know that Felipe would not accompany her, but it was he who insisted upon helping her on with her gear and checking it before she entered the water.

This time Julie had no fear of the hidden depths, for Felipe's tuition had given her confidence. It was then Felipe gave his instructions. Julie was to stay in the vicinity of the boat while he went off with Roddy. Sharon was to look after her.

The arrangement suited Julie since she was still a novice, but Sharon took it with a bad grace. She gave in sulkily, making no secret of her disappointment at not going with Felipe.

Julie found it sheer bliss to weave in and out of the underwater wonder world of sea life resembling cacti, and the changes of light and shade rippling through the depths intrigued her. She was so entranced that she did not notice Sharon's absence for some time.

Julie wondered if Sharon was hiding to tease when she had been searching around for some time without success. But Sharon was hardly the teasing kind, at least not to Julie Denver. Some sixth sense had told her from the very beginning that Sharon had resented her joining them. Julie considered the thought that she could have gone on ahead and she continued in that direction for some time.

After a while she discovered that in order to avoid obstacles in her way it was necessary to go down deeper in the water. There were more rocks about now and a sense of danger took hold as the water became a deeper blue. It was becoming colder all the time. There was still no sign of Sharon and when something cold brushed against her Julie looked for a clear way overhead to the surface. Her heart was pounding as she tried not to take in too much air and it was a relief when someone came swiftly towards her.

Sharon at last, she thought with a sigh of relief. But it was not Sharon who gripped her arm and forced her upwards to the surface. Felipe hauled her into the boat and she took off her mask with shaking fingers. If she had been scared just now in the water, she was even more scared by the look on Felipe's face as he freed it from his mask.

'Who do you think you are? Jacques Cousteau?' he demanded furiously. 'Sharon has been worried out of her mind because she lost you. Fortunately she knew where to contact us and she came right away.'

Julie accepted the rebuke gallantly, admitting that it was her own fault. She had been carried away by the beauty of it all. But she failed to see how Sharon could have lost her, since her progress through the water had been very slow.

'I'm sorry, Felipe,' she said, glad that the other two hadn't witnessed the rebuke.

The cold water in the depths of the sea had really chilled her and she was shivering as he worked quickly to free her.

In a voice that sounded strangely thick, he was saying, 'You went out of your depth, which is why you are shivering. You could have had cramp with the cold and sunk down among the rocks—then what would I have had to say to your father?'

She said humbly, 'I'm so sorry.'

He gave her a towel. 'Do not upset yourself. I will get something to warm you up. Rub yourself briskly and dress.'

Julie was in the blue linen again when he came with a glass.

'Drink this up,' he ordered.

She sipped part of the liquid that ran like fire through her veins.

'Warmer?' he asked, and smiled.

Julie nodded, feeling decidedly strange now the trembling had stopped. She nodded.

'You might have lost your life,' he said. 'Promise that you will not be so foolish again?'

Huskily, she said, 'I promise. I trust I haven't spoiled your fun?'

'You would have spoiled more than my fun had anything happened to you. Never explore treacherous places on your own.'

Julie nodded and he smiled again. His dark face was very near. The water glistened on his skin, his teeth looked very white.

Sharon was the first to clamber on to the boat. She gave them both a rapier-like glance and said pettishly, 'Where have you been, Julie? I've looked all over for you.' She shook her hair back, taking off her gear. 'Good thing I knew where to find Felipe and Roddy.'

Julie felt her colour rise. She was shaken by the edge on Sharon's voice. 'I suppose we just missed each other.'

Felipe said quietly, "One certainly cannot say that life is boring. Julie has made her presence felt in more ways than one.'

Julie turned her head to see that he was laughing at

her, but not unkindly.

'I have?' she queried.

'But certainly. Roddy is very shy of *señoritas*, yet with you he has been completely relaxed. Is that not so, Roddy?'

He looked beyond Julie to bestow a smile on Roddy's high colour.

'Yes,' Roddy admitted. 'I felt instantly at home with Julie when we first met. You are going out with us this evening, aren't you, Julie?'

With an inward tremor she felt a longing to be drawn into, yet escape from, she knew not what. The appeal in Roddy's nice brown eyes, his boyishness, melted away all her excuses for not doing so. It was not Roddy who bothered her but Felipe. So far she had only been a trouble to him, and if he did not appear to mind, she did.

Against Roddy's immaturity, Felipe made every nerve in her body aware of him. Long legs stretched out non-chalantly beside her, his long fingers curled around his drink, he was waiting for her answer.

'I'd love to,' she said.

They drove into Palma that evening for dinner. The road through unknown country was more lovely than Julie had recalled on coming to the hotel from the airport. She gazed out on an entrancing view of the town, finding it all the more interesting and exciting because she was with Felipe. She had completely forgotten Roddy sitting beside her.

Turning her head as she felt his eyes upon her, she found him studying her intently. The colour rode roughshod beneath his skin as their eyes met.

'Hi, Roddy,' she said, squeezing his hand.

'Hi, Julie,' he replied on a grin as his fingers closed around hers.

It was like shaking hands on a pact of friendship.

If only it could be like that with Felipe, she thought,
then gave up her silly fancies and looked forward to a
pleasant evening.

The night spot Felipe had chosen was a popular one
patronised by a select clientele, La Paloma. The sign
over the portals gleamed softly in lights and the door-
man was immaculate in his uniform.

Inside they were relieved of their wraps and shown
to a secluded table in a corner with a full view of the
room. The meal was excellent. The gazpacho, an An-
dalucian soup flavoured slightly with garlic, was delicious, so was the paella, a mixture of meat and shellfish
on a bed of saffron-flavoured rice. The cold meats,
salad and fruit which followed were all beautifully
presented.

By the time they had reached the coffee stage, Julie
was finding the food and drink combined with Felipe's
presence a little heady.

He leaned her way as Sharon said something to
Roddy.

'Enjoying it?' he asked.

'Very much,' she replied. 'It's been a wonderful
day.'

She laughed softly and happily, feeling strange beneath his scrutiny. The subdued lighting highlighted
the clear-cut planes of his face, the deep disturbing
look in his dark eyes.

'It is good to see you enjoying yourself. We must
make you laugh more often,' he murmured.

'Do I look so unhappy?' she said lightly.

He shrugged wide shoulders. 'There are many moments when you have the look of a lost child. Was your
childhood a happy one?'

'Wonderful.' Julie shone up at him, warmed by
memories so precious, so poignantly sweet because
they had gone never to return. Her voice was flippant.

'Too bad we have to grow up.'

He frowned. 'Surely growing up brings other delights to take the place of childhood joys? Marriage, children, for instance?'

In that moment a hush fell on the room and lights were lowered as a spotlight focussed on the centre of the cleared space for the evening's entertainment. Felipe offered cigarettes, and Julie declined with the feeling that she had missed something dangerous by the sudden termination of their conversation.

She did not flatter herself that Felipe was interested in her personally. He was only being polite. Why then was she so concerned as to where their conversation had been leading? Was it because she was in danger of becoming too interested in a man who had a different set of values from her own?

She gazed at the long brown fingers passing around the silver cigarette case, well cared for hands. How many women had they caressed? Mentally, Julie shrugged off the thought as being no concern of hers and noticed with quickening interest as he offered Sharon one of her American cigarettes. Roddy declined, saying that he preferred a cigar.

Felipe's black silky brows lifted a fraction at his request and regarded him with amused tolerance.

'You are sure you want a cigar, *amigo*?' he asked.

Roddy nodded while blushing slightly and Sharon stared at him indignantly.

'He's never had a cigar,' she cried. 'My little brother is showing off in front of Julie.'

'That's not true!' Roddy cried indignantly. 'I'm nineteen.'

Felipe's well-cut mouth quirked at the corners. 'Almost ancient,' he murmured, and passed Roddy a cigar. Then he clipped off the end of one for himself and provided a lighter.

Roddy accepted a light with bravado and proceeded to inhale from his cigar, his cheeks bulging out as he tried not to cough.

Julie was all for Roddy making a success of his cigar because she knew that it was important to his pride. It was all part of his growing up. Her eyes must have been giving him her support, for inadvertently she turned to Felipe for help, only to find him with the same expression in his eyes as he studied the boy.

The next moment Felipe had caught her gaze in a kind of telepathy that was both breathtaking and frightening. There was compassion in his face linked with a clear understanding of her feelings towards Roddy. Their eyes locked and her heart responded to him. It seemed that she was handing it to him on a plate. Feelings overwhelmed her. Steady on, you idiot! she admonished herself. He probably regards you as a juvenile who needs help as well.

There was movement and her attention was drawn to the centre of the room to where two performers in Spanish dress stood poised dramatically in the spotlight. A guitar twanged, and the dancers moved as one, slim, lissom and graceful, bowing, swaying to the music like saplings in the breeze. Each movement was poetry, every line of their bodies in an accord of perfect symmetry.

The man reminded Julie of Felipe, tall, dark, excitingly male with a leashed vitality that reached out to every woman in the audience. The music was swelling in intensity, gathering flute-like murmurs which came and went in exciting cadences, sweeping the audience along with them.

The dancers gave the impression of being alone, and dancing only for each other. The audience loved it. Insensibly through the medium of their art the dancers made their presence felt emotionally. Julie recognised it as art in its truest sense in a miracle of movement, an ineffable feeling of great joy in each magnificent gesture. As the dance drew to its dramatic climax excitement rippled around the room from a keyed-up audience. So great was their concentration that when the dance ended there was a second or so of uncanny silence. Flung from such emotional heights, they were moments before they reached the earth again.

Julie drew in a deep breath like one coming out of a trance and joined in the applause, which was deafening. The lights came on and she blinked at poor Roddy's face. It was a pale green. Felipe was on his feet in an instant and gently leading Roddy from the room.

Sharon watched them go with a disdainful curl of her lip.

Triumphantly, she said, 'I knew he'd be sick. He's a fool, showing off like that.'

'Aren't you being just a little hard on your brother?' Julie asked lightly. 'After all, he did take a challenge. He probably knew the cigar would make him sick, but he tried all the same. As an adolescent, Roddy is no exception. Boys like to show off their maturity in different ways. Girls look more grown up by using make-up. Boys can't do that, so they try something else like smoking cigars.'

Sharon let this pass and said pompously, 'I don't know what Felipe must think. Really, it's so embarrassing!'

Julie laughed at her stuffiness. 'I bet Felipe is enjoying it. He might have gone through a similar experience at Roddy's age himself.'

Sharon sighed. 'I hope you're right. I don't want things to go wrong where Felipe is concerned. I'm very fond of him and my parents are too. He's coming to the States again to stay with us and I can't wait to show him off to my friends. He's so handsome and exciting, I can't wait!'

Looking at the glowing face, Julie felt a hundred years old, though there could have only been a few years between them.

'How old are you, Sharon?' she asked.

'Seventeen, nearly eighteen.'

'Have you a boy-friend back home?'

She laughed. 'Felipe is my boy-friend.'

'No one else back home?'

'No steady date, if that's what you mean. Felipe has spoiled me for anyone else. Who wants anything to do with boys like Roddy? Beside them Felipe is so experienced, so exciting.'

'Naturally. He can give you at least ten years,' Julie said dryly.

'Which is one of the reasons why he's so exciting. Don't you think? We met him in the States last year and I persuaded my parents to bring me here to see his home. The attraction is mutual, since he's hinted that he'll be seeing us again later in the States.'

Julie gazed at her, seeing a girl who had been brought up with everything she wanted. She could have been looking on a carbon copy of herself before her parents' divorce. She had grown up more in the last two years than most girls do in a lifetime. Gone were any delusions of being swept off her feet by some knight in shining armour. Too many doubts beset her mind now regarding the durability of marriage.

She was not seeing Felipe through rose-coloured spectacles like Sharon. Fair enough, there was something about him that struck an answering chord in her heart, but as she was the only one who was aware of it nothing would come of it. And here was Sharon starry-eyed over a dream. Surprised at her own cynicism, Julie hoped that fate would let Sharon down lightly.

Felipe returned with a pale edition of Roddy and soon they were on their way back home. She squeezed Roddy's hand as he sat pale and silent beside her and tried to banish a sensation of weariness. She had experienced too many emotions during the day and those last moments of soul-searching were making themselves felt.

Her unfailing response to Felipe's presence brought new problems and some disquiet. She was not sure how to fight his fascination or whether she could do anything about it at all.

She sat silent for the most part during the journey, turning things over in her mind, placing her feelings for Felipe on a slab, as it were, and clinically dissecting them.

She came to no conclusion other than deciding to keep out of Felipe's way as much as possible during her visit to the island.

The night was warm and still as they drove up hill and down dale at a pleasant speed. They were nearing the end of their journey when Sharon said, 'Do let's visit a bodega in the town for a nightcap, Felipe. I like the local wine and it will finish off our evening.'

Without slowing down Felipe said smoothly, 'I think not. The last thing Roddy wants at the moment is wine. I am taking you back to the farm.'

It was not Sharon's day, Julie thought wryly as she peered through the window at the unfamiliar road they were taking. If Felipe had intended to drop her off first at the Hotel Jacarandas then he was going the wrong way. She did not speak, however, since it was unlikely that Felipe had forgotten her presence in the car.

Presently they left the main highway behind and

were cruising along a narrower road lined with rocks
and shrubs. This led upwards winding in a way that
to Julie was exciting. Was she going to see the farm,
and did he intend to ask her in?

The road seemed to go on and on before they turned
into a kind of courtyard. Felipe stopped the car behind another already parked there and turned to
Sharon.

'You do not have to tell your parents about Roddy.
It was nothing,' he said, turning to bestow a smile on
her brother and Julie in the back of the car.

'How are you feeling, Roddy?' he asked.

'Fine. Sorry for making a fool of myself.'

'You did not,' Felipe assured him laconically. 'I
trust you all enjoyed the evening?'

Felipe had got out of the car and was going round
to help Sharon out when Roddy whispered urgently in
Julie's ear.

'Will you come out with me tomorrow, Julie?'

She hesitated, hating to disappoint him. But if she
was to keep her distance with Felipe it would be foolish to see Roddy again until she was sure that he
would not include her in any outings for the four of
them like today.

She said swiftly in an undertone, 'I'll telephone you.'

Felipe did not attempt to help her from the car. He
waited for Roddy to get out and bade them both
adios. Then he was back in the driving seat to reverse the car and drive away at speed.

If Julie was a little puzzled as to why he had not
dropped her off at the Hotel Jacarandas, she did not
comment. On an island as small as this it could not have
taken him much out of his way to do so. She would
have liked to have seen his farm, though.

He drove some way in silence. Then, 'There are two
things I want to do before taking you back to your

hotel. One is to show you the view of Palma by night, the other to take you to a bodega to try the local wine.'

He was slowing down and turning the car off the road on to a kind of plateau.

'The one goes with the other,' he said, helping her from the car. 'The mountain air is crisp and cool at night and a glass of wine will warm you up after our small stroll to the bodega.'

Taking her elbow into a warm protective grip, he led her to the edge of the plateau to look over the plains towards Palma. It was not quite dark on a beautiful summer evening, and as the moon washed the island in several degrees of light and shade there was only one word for it—idyllic.

Standing there with Felipe looking over the undulating plains towards Palma shrouded a little in night mist, Julie had never been happier. She was in a dream as she gazed on the dream that was Palma. Above the city, the cathedral rose majestically to look over the silver waters of the Mediterranean. At intervals, in the hills, convents, churches and beautifully designed villas slumbered unspoiled.

Julie said impulsively and with feeling, 'I hope nothing ever happens to destroy what we're looking at now. So much destruction of beautiful buildings all over the world has gone on through the ages.'

Felipe agreed. 'Diabolical things have been done in the name of progress, which is bad in some ways when one has to sacrifice happiness to achieve it.'

Julie gave a sudden shiver in air that was cool after the confined space of the car. Instantly he put a gentle pressure on her arm for them to move on.

'Now you see why bodegas are so popular,' he teased in deep tones. 'After the heat of the day the night air needs a little bolstering.'

The small village they strolled through lay neat and

inviting in the stillness. Shops slumbered behind
shutters and houses displayed plaques of their favourite saint beside their front doors. The bodega was
quaint and the low beamed ceiling sheltering rough
hewn tables and chairs gave the impression that a
landlord would appear in knee-breeches and cravat.
Settles nestled against white walls and a log fire burned
in a Spanish fireplace at the far end of the room, giving off a pleasant smell of pine.

Felipe steered Julie into a corner in the chimney
breast and the landlord brought them wine.

'Do you like it?' Felipe asked.

He watched her as she sipped the wine, which to her
had a pleasing bouquet that entirely agreed with her
palate. The matured golden liquid slid down her
throat like nectar from the gods—and all because she
was with Felipe.

'It's delicious,' she replied, savouring it with relish.
'Is it very old?'

'Our local brew, made with grapes from my vineyards,' he replied.

'Really?' she smiled. 'Then it has to be good.'

She laughed softly, feeling idiotically happy, and he
laughed with her, his teeth showing up the darkness of
his tan. For blissful moments the barriers were down
between them and they were just another couple enjoying a last drink at the bodega before saying goodnight. Felipe told her how the wine was made and
how important it was to the islanders since it acted as
food and drink to them in the winter months.

She could have sat there all night listening to the deep
cadences of his voice, there in the cosy nook with the
firelight flickering on his dark features, and the ring
on his finger as he held his glass to catch the light. She
thought—to share all my evenings with him like this;
to sit back against him at his feet beside the fire with

his hand on my hair. She trembled, realising that it was
something she wanted above all else.

It was there to stay, this feeling for one man above
all others. It was no romantic whim any more than
it was fascination for good looks and charm. There
was something more, something as shattering as it was
hopeless, and there was nothing that she could do
about it. She was in love, really in love, for the first
time in her life.

Julie wanted her glass of wine to last for ever. It
was not fair, she argued, that such a wonderful moment of enlightenment should be so brief, that Felipe
did not share her own feelings of a wonderful discovery.

Instead he spoke about the beauty spots on the
island which she had to see during her holiday.

'You must go to see the Cuevas del Drach near to
the charming little town of Porto Cristo. I still recall
the magic of my visits there as a child.'

She said, 'Have you always lived on the island?'

'No. The family home is in Cadiz. I spent my holidays here with my grandparents.'

'How nice for a place as beautiful as this to hold
such happy memories for you,' she said, at the same
time envying the island because it had known him for
far longer than she had.

'I trust the island will hold happy memories for you
also,' he assured her.

She learned that his grandparents had left him the
farm and that his real home was still in Cadiz. At last
they rose to go and Julie wondered if Felipe was as
reluctant to go as she was. She knew he was not so
lightheaded. She might have drunk a bottle of wine she
was so bemused as they went back to his car.

This time he put her into the front seat beside him,
and they drove back to the hotel almost in silence.

The wine had warmed her to a rosy glow and she was feeling dreadfully sleepy. It was an effort to keep her eyes open and she felt the desire to yawn more than once. She had eaten too well and the wine at the bodega had indeed been a nightcap.

At the entrance to the hotel Felipe handed her from the car.

'Thank you for giving me an unforgettable day.' Julie almost swayed with tiredness as she spoke, but the need to be awake and polite was strong.

'You enjoyed it?'

'Very much.'

In the half light with his back to the lighted hotel entrance, his eyes looked very dark and there was something in his expression which made her feel weak and uncertain.

His eyes narrowed on the aura of tawny hair and the sleepy brown eloquent eyes. Then he smiled.

'We must repeat our day again quite soon. *Hasta la vista*, Julie. Sleep well.'

'*Hasta la vista*, Felipe,' she replied, smiling up at him drowsily.

He hesitated for a moment, about to say something. The moment passed and he made a polite gesture of farewell. Without looking round Julie knew that he was standing where she had left him watching her enter the hotel.

CHAPTER FOUR

JULIE breathed deeply, taking in the exciting freshness
of a new day. Below her window men were at work in
the grounds cleaning out the swimming pool and setting up loungers to greet the sun. The mirror in her
bathroom had shown her a face glowing with health,
her new tan giving her the look of a ripening peach.

She stretched her arms luxuriously above her head,
telling herself that the island was a wonderful place for
a holiday and to bless her luck in being there. She
looked longingly towards the hills in the direction of
Felipe's farm. Was he up yet on this gorgeous morning?

A tap on her door admitted Lucia with her breakfast tray.

'Buenos dias, miss. I have brought you fresh *ensaimadas* with honeycomb. They are delicious and one
of our favourite offerings for breakfast.'

The *ensaimadas*, sugar-coated, crisp and brown,
were as delicious as they looked and the honeycomb
was like nectar. Julie ate with relish, enjoying the
creamy coffee, at a loss to know who had ordered breakfast to be brought to her room so early.

She was soon to know. She had washed and dressed
when Dale came into her room clad in riding clothes.

'Enjoy your breakfast?' she asked with a smile as she
sat on the bed. 'I ordered it to be sent to you because
I thought you'd enjoy a ride this morning before it
gets too warm.'

Julie gazed down doubtfully at her slacks and sleeveless top, having promised herself a lazy morning on

54

the beach swimming when she felt like it and sun-bathing in between.

Without much enthusiasm, she said, 'I haven't any riding things and I haven't ridden for some time.' She almost added that she had done no riding since their friendship had broken up. But it was too painful to talk about when the reason for it breaking up had been Dale going away with her father. Julie was also reluctant to renew her friendship with Dale, feeling that it was disloyal to her mother. She was quite willing to be pleasant, but that was all.

Dale, however, was insistent. 'Those slacks will be fine. Come on,' she pleaded. 'I want you to meet José. He runs a riding school. Actually the stables belong to Felipe, who lets them to him. José is hoping to own his own place someday.'

Still Julie hesitated as she searched in a drawer for a fresh handkerchief.

'How do we get there? Is it far?'

'I have my car. So if you're ready, let's go.'

Dale was far too eager for Julie's liking, but she gave in, partly because she was curious about José and partly because Felipe owned the premises. Tying a scarf around her hair, she picked up her shoulder bag.

The hotel foyer was teeming with new arrivals and amid a hive of activity and clamour Julie saw her father conversing with their courier. He lifted a hand to her and she thought how tired he looked.

They were leaving the hotel when she paused. 'Daddy looks awfully busy. Should we stay to help, do you think?'

Dale laughed as if the question was absurd. 'Goodness, no! Ricky can cope.'

They had gone some distance in the car before Julie could reconcile herself to Dale's practical approach. Was it wishful thinking on her part that made her feel instinctively that her father was unhappy? She stared out on to endless vineyards to think this one out.

'This is Felipe's estate,' Dale explained. 'He does quite well in the wine trade and in the agricultural scene too.'

'Good for him,' Julie replied. 'He's smart.'

Dale said shortly, 'So is José, but he never seems to get on.'

Reasonably, Julie remarked, 'Maybe he doesn't go the right way about it.'

'He hasn't the money to back him like Felipe.'

'Money isn't always necessary to success.' Julie countered, with the feeling that if José scowled a bit less he might get somewhere. It was easy to see whose side Dale was on.

'José has the responsibility of looking after his aunt, Doña Conchita,' Dale continued.

Julie stared at Dale's unyielding profile. 'But surely his aunt has money to pay for any attention she needs?' she commented, with the lady's devoted maid in mind.

'Yes, but José is responsible for her.'

He's also her heir, Julie thought wryly, which meant that he had not to put a foot wrong if he wanted it to remain that way. She noticed that the vineyards had now given way to agricultural land and guessed that they were nearing their destination.

It was then that she saw the people on horseback, five of them in the distance to her right. She recognised Felipe immediately on a magnificent bay horse. He rode as though born to it. His companions were the Americans, all four of them.

Julie was relieved to have missed them and eyed the first of several long sprawling buildings through the trees. Dale pulled in at a courtyard lined on two sides with horse-boxes and on the third with barns containing feeding stuffs and farm implements. As they left the car a man in riding breeches appeared at the door of what looked like a small office next to the barns.

José would have looked attractive with his dark arresting looks and strong physique if only he had looked more friendly. He had neither Felipe's charm nor ease of manner, and she wondered what Dale saw in him.

Dale's reaction to his appearance was truly remarkable. She seemed to come to life all at once. Her cheeks glowed and her eyes shone as she greeted him.

'*Buenos dias*, José,' she cried gaily, going up to him. 'Can you find a mount for Julie?'

His dark eyes raked Julie's slacks and sleeveless top disdainfully before he strode to the horse-boxes, where he spoke to someone inside the second one. The next moment he was leading a horse towards them, followed by a boy carrying a saddle. José took the saddle from the boy and dismissed him with an arrogant gesture.

Dale moved forward immediately to caress the rich brown satin neck of the chestnut. 'You're honoured, Julie,' she observed. 'Damisela is one of José's favourites.'

Julie fondled the soft nose as José tightened the saddle, then he was giving her a leg up. Damisela was easy to ride and cavorted gently. Dale mounted an equally fine horse and they rode off together.

It was a beautifully sunny morning with a slight breeze, ideal weather for riding. Soon Julie was enjoying herself. Damisela whinneyed her delight as she kept up a long rhythmic stride, and negotiated without mishap any obstacles which lay in her path. Julie had taken off her head scarf and the wind lifted her tawny hair. Her cheeks glowed and her eyes were clear and bright.

They had been out an hour, had a rest dismounting by a brook to water the horses and were returning to the stables when Julie heard Dale give an exclamation of dismay.

'Oh lord! Look who's coming this way,' she exclaimed. 'I hardly think he's coming to see me, so I'm going to vamoose. See you later at the stables.'

Dale had gone so quickly that Julie was a while taking in the rider who was now quite near. Quelling the unruly beating of her heart, she put on a smile.

'*Buenos dias*, Felipe.'

His magnetic gaze was veiled and she felt instinctively that he hardly approved of her riding get-up. It was impossible not to reflect upon his smiling charm. Undoubtedly, he was a man who dressed correctly for every occasion and saw no reason why other people should not do the same.

His smile was faintly mocking. The immaculate riding jacket, polished boots and elegantly knotted silk cravat at his firm brown throat enhanced his charm, and poor Julie took a tight rein on her emotions.

'*Buenos dias*, Julie,' he answered. 'Why did you not mention yesterday that you wished to go riding? You could have accompanied my guests and myself. Roddy would have been delighted.' His eyes narrowed from her glowing face to the chestnut. 'I see you are riding Damisela, an excellent choice since, translated, the word means fine, young ... like yourself.'

'Thank you. I had no idea I would be going riding until Dale asked me to accompany her this morning.'

The well-cut mouth looked a trifle hard despite the charming smile.

'I observed her riding away just now,' he said with a hint of satire. 'Are you and Dale very close?'

'We ... we were friends before ... we worked at the same bank in London.'

Julie fixed her eyes on the signet ring on his hand

lightly holding the reins, feeling uncomfortable beneath his scrutiny. She upbraided herself for shying away from mentioning her father's involvement with Dale. It was taking her a long time to live with it, but there it was still very painful to talk about.

A brief silence, then she might have known that those dark intelligent eyes missed nothing.

'It must be painful for you, this break-up of your parents?'

He did not wait for an answer, adding carelessly, 'Riding is an excellent way to see the island. I would be interested to hear your views on it along with those of my American guests. Their views are so refreshingly frank. On the other hand, they have seen so much of the world that their views, at times, are a trifle jaded.'

They were riding back to the farm at a slow pace and Julie knew that sybaritic bliss of living just for the moment. She was riding with the handsomest and most exciting man she had ever met and she found herself smiling idiotically at her own good fortune.

She said lightly, 'I suppose it depends upon what kind of mood your American friends are in when you ask their opinion. Sometimes no matter how beautiful a place is it can be spoilt for ever by some unpleasant or disturbing little incident.'

He looked at her sharply. 'Has any such incident happened to you since you arrived?'

'None at all.'

'But you have reservations. Your family?'

Julie bit on her lip. 'I'd rather not talk about it. No one can begin to understand another person's motives unless they've been in a similar position themselves,' she said stiffly.

'True,' he conceded dryly. 'Your father is a fine man. Even so, I do not condone what he has done. Were I

married I certainly would not attempt to solve my
marital differences by seeking a divorce. I would not
let my wife go so easily.'

He sounded so arrogant, so sure of his own charms
that Julie was stung to protest.

'You might have no other choice if you were married
to an English girl,' she said lightly.

'Nothing is further from my mind. If I did I would
deserve all I got from such a union. Fortunately that
is not likely to happen.'

Julie glanced at him sitting straight in the saddle
with that ease of movement that was inherent in him.
She could believe what he said. He was the kind of
man who would wear the trousers in his own household. His imperious manner had been nurtured
throughout his life; he was a man who would keep
his household in order and his wife in her place.

A Spanish woman would not question his right to
do so, might even derive a certain amount of enjoy-
ment from it. Life with Felipe de Torres y Aquiliño
would never be dull. Julie imagined those long brown
fingers caressingly gentle or tightening with a possessive
grip and she quivered at the thought.

Come, come, she said to herself. This isn't love but
infatuation for a handsome man of infinite charm
who's intriguing because he's a foreigner. Many girls
must have fallen for his charms and many more would.
Julie Denver was just another idiot who was too
romantic for her own good.

Julie did not know whether she was glad or sorry
to see the stables coming into view. She only knew that
his nearness was suffocating and she had to go away
to think. The big bay horse stopped at the arched gate-
way leading to the stables and Felipe looked down at
her.

'I have a small party this evening and we plan to go

on to a *fiesta* in town. Would you join us?'

'That's very kind of you and I appreciate it. Some other time, perhaps,' she said politely.

His eyes narrowed. Julie had the feeling that he did not care for the brush-off.

'I'm sorry you are unable to join us. You would have enjoyed it. Meanwhile, enjoy your day.' There was a pause. Then he added carelessly, 'And your evening. *Buenos dias*, Julie.'

He had gone before she could reply. Dale came out of the office as she dismounted in the courtyard. There was no sign of José.

'Has the great man gone?' asked Dale, flipping a cool finger in the direction of the farm.

Julie nodded. 'He doesn't stable his horse here then?' she said curiously.

'He has his own stables at the farm,' said Dale as José came from the office to take Damisela's bridle.

'Did you enjoy your ride, *señorita*?' he asked.

'Very much, thank you. And thank you for giving me your Damisela to ride. I must pay for the privilege,' Julie said firmly. 'How much do I owe you?'

She withdrew some money from the pocket of her slacks put there for the purpose, but José ignored her outstretched hand and called the boy to take the horse to its box.

His action made her all the more determined to pay for her pleasure since it would, to her way of thinking, be out of the question to receive any favours from this surly man. She gave the money to the boy, emphasising her action by closing her hand over his. He gave her a wide delighted smile, and she was aware of Dale's laugh.

Dale said as they walked to the car, 'What was all that about? I told you José expects no payment from us. He regards you as family.'

'That isn't the way I see it,' Julie protested as lightly as she could. 'There's no reason why I shouldn't pay for my ride.'

Dale took her up on it with another light laugh. 'Then next time I suggest you go riding with Felipe. That way there would be no question of you paying for your ride—and don't tell Ricky. He's done a lot for José and he wouldn't like it, and you did come at my invitation. The important thing is did you enjoy it? After all, you had one of the best mounts in the stable.'

Julie assured her that she had. She told herself not to mind Dale in her present mood, for she was not sure if she was putting on an act or not. In the first place she had not been too happy over the invitation to go riding with her. Julie had the feeling that Dale was not as friendly as she was making out. Her apprehension could have something to do with the surly José. Whatever it was Julie maintained the restraint she felt for the journey back, keeping the conversation superficial.

She had a word with her father who was talking to Tomas at the reception desk upon their return to the hotel. He told her that Roddy had called that morning just after she had left the hotel and he had called again only half an hour ago.

Julie said she would make the call in her room and went in that direction, relieved to see that her father looked brighter. She washed and changed into a pretty sun-dress before telephoning Roddy. She apologised for not being in when he had called, but as she was on holiday this was hardly surprising. She thanked him for telephoning, but the next few days would be fairly hectic ones and she would let him know when she was free.

She put down the telephone feeling mean, but it was mingled with a sense of freedom. She was fast becoming too involved with other people and it was leading to that loss of insouciance, the boundless expectation of a holiday free from stress.

Julie had lunch with her father and Dale with the head waiter hovering like a mother hen. Julie had a rapport with Jaime from the start. He was a slight man with well brushed dark hair and immaculate appearance. Like Tomas on reception, he was easy to know. Julie noticed that her father had the same friendly relationship with all his staff. They all appeared to adore him.

Dale left them after lunch to spend an hour or so on reception. Her father lit a cigar and asked how her holiday was progressing. If he had any reservations at having asked her to come he made no mention of them.

'What about this boy Roddy?' he asked. 'Bit young for you, isn't he? He was very disappointed to find you out when he telephoned. Got anyone in mind to spend the rest of your life with yet?'

'There's no one,' she answered, ignoring a tantalising picture of loose-limbed grace and dark eyes in her mind. 'I came to see my dear father and to have a holiday. I plan on doing just that. I'm going down to the beach this afternoon to swim and sunbathe.'

He blew out a line of cigar smoke and eyed her affectionately.

'I worry about you. But I'm glad you have more pride and self-respect than to live with a man out of wedlock. The trouble is I know no man is half good enough for you.'

She laughed. 'Oh, Daddy, you are funny! I suppose I shall fall in love some day regardless of what the man is or has.'

Hastily she changed the subject, with a desire to rid herself of Felipe's darkly handsome face mocking her.

'How are you coping with your guests?' she said over the last of her coffee, and loving these precious moments with him. 'I want to help in any way I can, so let me know if there's anything I can do.'

His eyes twinkled. 'Stop fretting that pretty head of yours over something that isn't happening. Everything is under control. It's the unexpected which is really something to look forward to. Without that our lives would be very dull indeed.'

'I suppose you're right,' Julie agreed with a sigh. 'The staff seem to be content. There's a pleasant atmosphere pervading the hotel.'

He nodded, pulling contentedly on his cigar. 'I've been lucky with my staff. By the way, I'm going out to dine this evening with a friend. Like to come along? Dale will be staying in to keep an eye on things.'

'A friend?' Julie queried with bated breath.

'A bank manager transferred from London to the island.'

'Anyone I know?'

'No, and he isn't married. Interested?'

'Oh, Daddy!' she cried in mock dismay. 'You never give up, do you? No, thanks. I'm staying in to wash my hair.'

'Suit yourself. But if you change your mind ...'

'I shan't,' she replied, and he laughed.

It was bliss that afternoon on the beach. Julie swam for a long time, then lay on her towel to fall fast asleep. Some sixth sense awakened her and she opened her eyes to screw them up against the brightness and saw someone looking down at her. Roddy's look of appraisal at her recumbent form in the brief swimsuit did much to take the ire from her anger at finding him there.

'For goodness' sake, Roddy ...' she began shortly.

'I hope you don't mind,' he said a little shyly. 'I

telephoned Dale and she told me where to find you.'

Julie sat up and reached for her wrap which she slid into as he dropped down beside her on the sand.

She said crossly, 'Dale had no business to tell you my whereabouts. I wanted the afternoon on my own. Besides, what about your family? Surely they want you with them?'

He looked sheepish. 'Dad is with Felipe on the farm and Mother has gone shopping in Palma with Sharon.'

'Leaving you alone?' she queried in disbelief. 'Really, Roddy, you can do better than that!'

He shrugged. 'Is it a crime to want to see you again? I'll go if you want me to.'

She stared at him in bewilderment, wondering what she had let herself in for. Then she began to laugh and he laughed too.

'Oh, Roddy,' she cried, 'whatever am I going to do with you? You haven't the least idea how to set about starting a friendship with a girl. You ought to have begun by saying something like, "What a surprise seeing you here!" It's a naïve approach, but at least it's better than making yourself so transparent. Watch Felipe in his approach to women. He's a man of experience. Women love to be wooed with just that subtle bit of command which is sheer romance in its approach. In these enlightened days women can sense a tenderfoot and treat him accordingly.'

Julie tied the cord of her wrap and settled down into a sitting position beside Roddy to hug her knees.

'Do you like Felipe?' he asked, turning towards her as he lay full length to support himself on one elbow.

'I don't have to like him to know that he's sure-fire with the ladies, Roddy. Granted, the man has oodles of charm, but so have you if you use it. Never grovel or be humble with the opposite sex. Women love the arrogant virile male.'

Roddy gloomily scooped up a handful of sand, then flung it from him in disgust.

'And I thought I was getting along with you just fine,' he growled.

'So you are. You're a very nice boy, but you have a lot of growing up to do to catch up with me. I like you very much, despite the fact that you're much too young to consider forming any lasting attachment yet. I'm here on holiday. I enjoy your company, but not all the time.'

'I see. You want me to go now?'

'Of course not. I just want to get things clear, that's all.'

Julie felt sorry to see his downcast face and in a moment of compassion she leaned down to kiss his tanned cheek.

'I'll take you to the hotel for tea,' she said. 'You can tell me all about your friends in America.'

She dined with Dale at the hotel that evening. Her father had left to dine with his friend. Julie had promised herself an early night after washing her hair, but the evening air was so inviting with the cool sea breeze taking the sting out of the day's heat that she sat on the terrace for a while.

Elegantly gowned women and men in evening dress were arriving to converge upon the restaurant from all directions. There was a select clientele of non-residents who visited the hotel every night and it was interesting to watch them arrive.

Julie watched them, then stiffened as a tall figure appeared at the end of the terrace to walk towards her. Felipe. Her heart caught in her throat. She was aware with something of a shock of his Latin good looks in evening dress. There was a perceptible glitter in the dark eyes and he sounded distinctly alien when he spoke.

'*Buenas tardes*, Julie. Waiting for your escort for the evening?'

'I'm ... staying in with Dale,' she said on regained breath.

He frowned. 'I came to see your father. Do you know where he might be?'

'He's dining out this evening with a friend.'

'I see.'

'Is it important? Perhaps Dale could help you?'

'Like your father, Dale is nowhere around.'

'Oh dear. But she must be—we dined together just now. I'll go and look for her.'

His voice forestalled any move she might have made and he spoke with what Julie regarded unnecessary harshness.

'Dale is nowhere in the hotel. No need to look so shattered,' he said sardonically. 'The hotel practically runs itself. The staff here are fully trained.'

A nerve twitched near Julie's mouth. Should she smile? Would it ease the situation? Bother Dale! Where on earth could she be? Then a thought occurred to her.

'My father might have left a telephone number at the desk in case we wanted to get in touch with him.'

She rose to her feet as she spoke.

'Just a moment.' Felipe stopped her with a quiet air of command. 'I am taking my guests into Palma for the evening. We were dining at the farm, but my chef is indisposed and we came here on the offchance of getting a table, but they are all booked up. I could not put the staff to further inconvenience by booking a private room without warning. It would have been different had your father been here.'

'At least let me enquire at reception ...' Julie began, when someone joined them on the terrace.

Dale was out of breath and her hair was dishevelled.

She had the look of a girl who had been kissed rather thoroughly, Julie thought. She had not, of course, she told herself impatiently. It was just her romantic mind running away with her. Felipe again. Why did he have to be so handsome, so disturbing ... so everything?

His manner changed as he addressed her. '*Buenas tardes*, Dale. You are a little late. I have left my guests waiting for me long enough. *Buenas noches*, Dale, Julie.'

'What's the matter with him?' Dale asked indignantly on breath regained. 'And what did he mean about me being a little late?'

'His chef is ill and he brought a party here to dine before going to the *fiesta* in Palma. He was none too pleased to find that we were booked up and that both you and Daddy were missing,' Julie told her wryly.

Dale smoothed down her hair. 'Why should he be annoyed to find us out?' she cried in injured tones. 'We aren't here at his beck and call.'

'I agree,' Julie murmured. 'Where were you, by the way?'

'Around,' Dale replied vaguely, and turned on her heel to leave Julie staring after her.

Julie did wash her hair, but she was far too restless to settle down with a book after drying it. It was around eleven o'clock when she decided to go into the grounds for a breath of air before bed. The loveliness of the island, the sunshine and the comforts of the hotel were pleasures she was enjoying if only ... she shook herself out of thoughts much too unsettling and found herself on the terrace where she lingered for a few moments, then left because it was too full of the ghost of Felipe.

She was making her way back to her room when she met Dale on the corridor. There was a curious expression on her face, half fearful, half pleading.

'About this evening, Julie,' she began. 'Do me a favour and don't mention anything of Felipe coming to the hotel, will you? Ricky will be angry if he hears about it. He thinks a lot of Felipe. I should have been on duty when Felipe arrived, but I'd just slipped out.'

Julie frowned. 'I don't see why Daddy should be angry about it. You're entitled to slip out if you want to.'

'I know, but I think it will be better if Ricky isn't told. It isn't very often he goes out and I don't want him to know that he can't trust me to be in when I'm needed.'

Julie said brightly, 'Not to worry. I wasn't going to say anything to Daddy in any case. What's more, I don't think Felipe will mention it either.'

Later in her room Julie was still wondering about Dale. Did she slip out to see a lover? She doesn't know what love is, Julie thought bleakly. But did she know herself? What was it, an aching searing need for the arms of one particular person, the desire for a partner to combat the loneliness?

She had not put on the light and the room was filled with sweet elusive shadows when she climbed into bed. Lying there, it seemed to her that Felipe had destroyed the whole fabric of her life. Futile to deny how his touch thrilled and stirred her, and how easy it would be to succumb to the power he had over her senses. It wasn't as though they had anything in common. They spoke different languages and their way of living was different. Yet Julie knew that her life would never know fulfilment without him.

The disillusionment of her parents' divorce, her own consequent disbelief in connubial bliss, was all forgotten in this madness which possessed her. Love was not the calm kind of relationship she had witnessed in her youth between her parents. It was a fiercely rag-

ing torrent which carried one along on the crest of a
wave with no thought in the head except for the beloved.

The shrill ringing of the telephone beside her bed
startled her profoundly. It was Roddy.

'Hullo, Julie,' he cried, bright as a new penny. 'What
about doing something unusual tomorrow?'

'Like what?'

'Like going cycling around the island. There's a
place in the village where you can hire bikes.'

She had to smile. 'I could think of several good
reasons not to. First of all it's too warm and I haven't
ridden a bike in years.' She paused as the sense of adventure overtook her. 'Sounds fun, though. What if
it's raining?'

'It won't be. I'll pick you up at ten in the car and
we can go on to the village for our cycles.'

'Just like that,' she laughed. 'You're on!'

CHAPTER FIVE

HER father was delighted the next morning to hear that she was going cycling with Roddy.

'Don't overdo it,' he warned, eyeing her slacks and sleeveless top. 'I'll ring the kitchens to pack you some food, and keep an eye on the weather.'

When Roddy arrived Julie was ready with a swim-suit next to her skin and a box of food for a picnic. Her father waved them off like a couple of children and for the rest of the day they behaved like them.

Julie took to the cycle like a duck takes to water. Roddy fastened the picnic basket to the back of his and they set off over rough country. Despite bumps and dips Julie enjoyed it immensely. Brimful of the sense of adventure, she was content to let Roddy expel all thoughts of the absent Felipe.

They cycled leisurely for about an hour, then sat down to rest high above the sea and to eat a juicy peach from the picnic basket. Later they went down to the beach to plunge into the cool sea.

They swam, acted the fool and chased each other in the blue water for all the world like two children who had not seen the sea in years, doing acrobatic hand turns and playing leapfrog on the white sand, then cooling off by dips in the sea.

By lunch time they had worked up a good appetite and laid out their lunch in the shade of trees. The food was ambrosia—ham, chicken, cheese, fruit, olives, and nuts. There was a bottle of wine in a wicker basket. Replete with food, they lay on their backs in the sun to listen to the cries of children playing on the edge of the water.

There were only two families on the beach and the children were playing in a rubber dinghy. Lulled by the warm breeze and the wine, Julie closed her eyes and drifted into sleep. She was awakened by a plop of rain falling on her face and opened her eyes to squint through a closing curtain of it blotting out the sky.

She was up in a moment. 'Come on, Roddy!' she cried, putting on her sun-dress. 'It's raining!'

'Jumping cats,' he said, opening sleepy eyes and sitting up bemused.

'Come on,' Julie repeated urgently as she began to gather up the remains of the picnic.

By the time they had dressed and reached the spot where they had parked their cycles the rain had eased off, but the clouds still rumbled ominously.

A fitful sun highlighted cliffs plunging down to shimmering sands, and villas clung to steep slopes in moving light and shade as the clouds moved across the sun. While Roddy pumped up one of his cycle tires Julie gazed inland to where vineyards nestled.

'Roddy,' she asked curiously, 'is Felipe's estate somewhere over there beyond the vineyards?'

Roddy straightened from his task to follow her gaze.

'That's right,' he replied. 'If you look beyond the vineyards you can just about see the farm building among the trees.'

He went on with his task and Julie gazed across the vineyards to the roofs of the stables José rented. There were two riders emerging from trees making their way down a slope leading to a stream. The sun caught the water as Julie recognised them. Smote into stillness, she leaned against the sun-warmed rock to watch Dale's shapely form swaying closer to that of her companion.

He was hatless, but there was no mistaking the rough
black head of José.

They tethered their horses and began to stroll along
the side of the stream. It had all happened so quickly
that Julie felt she might have dreamed it if it had not
been for the tethered horses. So that was why Dale
had asked her to go riding with her! Not every day, of
course. It had to be occasionally, just enough to avoid
a breath of scandal reaching her father's ears.

Anger shook Julie from head to toe. Never for a moment did she put down their meeting as casual or un-
important. Roddy was now examining the tires on her
cycle and she stood tense, willing the two figures to
reappear. At last they came back to the horses and
Julie drew a deep breath. Steady on, she told herself.
They've done nothing wrong, not even kissed. José
might regard Dale as a friend to confide in, nothing
more.

But something dark blotted out the joy of her day
and as if to emphasise it the black clouds moved to
cover the sun. Julie shivered and Roddy had finished
pumping up the tires when the first drops of rain
came.

Dale and José were now standing by their horses
talking earnestly as Julie cast a last look their way. She
wanted to fly over the intervening space between them
and demand what kind of a game they were playing,
but instead she murmured something to Roddy about
the rain as they wheeled their cycles on to the road.

It was evidently a thunderstorm, the rain heavy and
prolonged, and they paused looking round for shelter.
Their path lay downhill, so they decided to go on for
a while hoping the rain would stop. The road was
rough and the blinding rain was a curtain they had to
peer through with drenched eyes.

It all happened with cataclysmic suddenness. Julie

did not know what had hit her. The front wheel of her
cycle had struck a stone in the appalling road and she
sailed over the handlebars to land heavily on the
ground. She lay there for several moments with the
breath knocked out of her, hands tingling, knees hurting.

Roddy was there in a flash to pick her up. 'Are you
all right, Julie?' he asked in concern. 'What happened?'

Julie clung to him for a moment bereft of speech,
thankful for the rain reviving her blurred senses. She
felt sick and perspiration oozed from her temples,
although she was feeling cold.

She said with a lighthearted attempt at mirth, 'I
hit a stone in the road. I'll be fine in a minute.'

Practically, Roddy said, 'Your hands are grazed. I'm
awfully sorry. It looks as if the front wheel of your
cycle is buckled.'

Julie laughed weakly. 'Job's comforter, aren't you?'
she quipped, and drew in several deep breaths.

The stuffing had been knocked out of her, but she
was beginning to come round. Mopping her wet face
and grazed hands while Roddy picked up her cycle,
she was moved to laughter at the sorry sight they made.
They were hardly recognisable with the rain flatten-
ing their hair and their clothes moulded to their
bodies.

But Roddy was not seeing the funny side. 'I'm sorry,
Julie,' he said. 'I've gotten you into this mess. It
wouldn't have happened if I hadn't suggested it in the
first place.'

She smiled at his American idiom. 'So what!' she exclaimed gallantly. 'We've had a smashing day out—
and smashing is the word! It seems I've smashed up my
cycle, but I'm feeling better every minute. So cheer up.'

She forced herself to be cheerful in order to bring a

smile to Roddy's downcast face. She was still feeling
sick and shaky, but it was bearable. A rumble of distant
thunder drew her eyes to the skies to see a definite
break in the clouds.

'The rain is abating,' she remarked cheerfully. 'We'd
better push on.'

Push was the word, she thought ruefully, as she gazed
at the buckled wheel. Roddy was examining it when
the sound of hooves came to their ears and a rider
loomed up before them.

'What is this? What has happened?' Felipe demanded.

He had dismounted and was staring at each be-
draggled figure as though he could not believe his
eyes as a second rider joined them—Roddy's father.

Roddy straightened from the cycle and pushed back
his wet hair from his face.

'Julie came off her cycle,' he said.

Felipe ignored the damaged cycle and moved in to
take hold of Julie's hands. His mouth thinned in anger
as he saw the mess they were in.

Julie was in a sorry state with the rain running down
her face, her clothes sticking to her and the tumble
making itself felt now that the numbness had worn
of. Events were crowding in on her so swiftly that she
was lost for words. It was the sight of Roddy's em-
barrassed face that brought back her speech.

'It was my fault,' she said, trying to forget where
she hurt most. She was beginning to tremble. 'It ... it
was the rain, you see.'

But Felipe was not listening. He was taking off his
jacket, wrapping her in it and lifting her on his horse.
Then he was leaping up behind her, leaving Roddy
and his father looking helplessly on as he rode away.

During that short silent journey Julie could only
conclude that Felipe had seen them while out riding

with Roddy's father. It would have to be Felipe, she
thought dismally. But the fact that he had found her
looking so awful faded into insignificance as she gradually began to lose interest in everything around her.

It was like taking part in some delirious dream
where even the bliss of being held in Felipe's arms did
not register. The pain from her grazed hands and
knees was making her feel sick.

She went hot and cold by turns and closed her eyes,
knowing that there was a limit to her endurance. The
horse slithered down hills, splashed through shallow
water and eventually clattered to a halt in a cobbled
courtyard.

Felipe said a few clipped words to someone who
came running, and lifted her down. Then he was carrying her indoors where they were met by a plump
matronly-looking woman whose dark eyes goggled
as he barked out orders.

After being lowered gently on a bed she was given
a perfectly revolting drink that strangely enough dismissed the nausea she had been plagued with. Some
time later she was sitting on a settee after seeing her
wet clothes being taken away and submitting to a
warm bath with the help of Felipe's housekeeper.

She was clad in clean underwear and a button-
through linen dress which she presumed belonged to
Sharon since they shared the same size in clothes. The
room was filled with sunlight. It thrust itself through
shutters drawn to keep out the day's heat, for the rain
had ceased and everywhere would be dry again in no
time.

The ceiling of the room was crissed-crossed in soft
dark wood, the walls were white and gave the room a
cloistered air, and Julie knew that this was Felipe's
home.

He came into the room bearing a bowl of warm water

that smelled faintly of antiseptic. He had washed and
changed into slacks and a white shirt. A silk cravat was
tucked in the neck of his shirt.

His touch was very gentle as he bathed her grazed
hands. Fortunately her slacks had protected her knees
which had only been bruised.

At first Julie looked anywhere other than straight
at him, at the floor covered with beautiful rugs, at the
gleaming copper overhead lamp, and the furniture
gleaming darkly against white walls.

'You are very pale, *pequeña*,' he observed.

His deep voice shattered her thoughts as he pressed
adhesive dressings on her palms.

'I'm fine now, thanks,' she assured him. 'That
draught you gave me did the trick. I'm so sorry to give
you so much trouble, when you've been so kind. I
hope poor Roddy managed to take the cycles back to
the village.'

He evidently did not share her sympathies for
Roddy, for his mouth thinned and he said icily, 'I
would say that it was poor Julie. Roddy escaped far too
lightly. Whatever possessed you to cavort around the
island on a cycle when you could have so easily had a
car? I will put one at your disposal.'

She met his dark gaze head on—a mistake since it
set her pulses racing.

'Cycling was fun,' she said, looking down at her hand
in his palm. 'We went for a picnic and a swim and I
had to spoil it all by hitting a stone in the road.'

There was a short silence while he studied her
downbent head. His voice was filled with disapproval.

'*Señoritas* do not usually prance around the countryside on cycles. Yet you confess to enjoying the experience.'

She laughed. 'Why not? Lots of girls cycle in London. We might all come to it if all the oil runs out.'

She drew her hand away from his warm hold as the
housekeeper entered the room with a covered tray.

The good lady had helped her shed her wet clothes
with a silence bristling with disapproval. It had been
obvious from the start that the whole event had
offended her sense of decorum. She placed the tray
down very formally, announced that she would inform
Julie when her clothes were dry and left the room with
dignity.

She ran a hand over hair that was drying soft and
silky and caught Felipe's glance.

'You have very beautiful hair,' he said, and she felt
the colour rush to her face beneath his scrutiny.

She was immediately conscious of a shiny nose and
a face free from make-up, and said the first thing that
came into her head.

'I never thought I'd be taking tea with you this afternoon.'

'You would enjoy it more with Roddy, perhaps?'

'Of course not. I was curious to see your home.'

His expression did not alter as he replenished her
cup and passed it to her. The fact that he had only
taken liquid refreshment himself had not escaped her,
and she wished with some degree of irritation that he
would nibble a pastry or something. His attitude gave
a slightly uneasy conventionness to what could have
been an enjoyable get-together.

'Your first visit here is not the one I would have
chosen, but there will be more,' he said.

Julie saw little likelihood of this, but was reluctant
for the afternoon to end. She thought of Roddy and
wondered how he had fared. They had evidently not
returned to the farm, or if they had they were not making it known.

She said, 'I hope Roddy won't get in trouble over
the cycle. I shall pay for the damage, of course.'

She glanced at him, then quickly away, as she saw the expression of displeasure on his face.

'Roddy has behaved irresponsibly and I blame him for your accident. Your injuries might easily have been much worse. There was the danger of riding over a cliff in your ignorance of the island. I want you to promise me that you will not go out with him again alone.'

His request was so unexpected, so unreasonable, that she stared at his set face wondering if she had heard aright.

'You can't be serious! I like Roddy. He's a little young, but he's fun to be with,' she replied, on the defensive.

He leaned forward and she was aware of the thickness of his dark eyelashes, the sensitive curve of his nostrils.

'So, Roddy is fun; your accident was fun; your grazed hands are fun? Today has been hilariously funny, no?'

'You know I didn't mean that. Roddy is only a boy. There's no reason why I shouldn't go out with him, and I'm surprised at you insisting that I don't. After all, you take his sister Sharon out and she's only seventeen.'

He said curtly, 'They are my guests. It is my duty to entertain them.'

'Which you do very well, I'm sure but you have no right to tell me who I go out with,' she told him gently.

'I do not agree. You have sustained an accident through one of my guests. Your father will not be very happy to learn of your accident.'

Julie said with dignity, 'Daddy will understand.'

'Which does not take the onus from me.'

'Agreed,' she answered, and hastily changed the subject. 'Thank you for bringing me here. I loved your horse. Do you breed them?'

'I have done. You would like to see my stables?'

She nodded eagerly. 'Yes, please.'

'Sure you feel up to it?'

Felipe held her arm lightly as they entered the
stables. It had been agony for her to rise from her
seat and set her legs in action, but she would have died
sooner than let Felipe see her discomfort.

There was a sweet smell of fresh hay. Against white-
washed walls leather harness hung and there was the
sound of hooves moving restlessly on the earth floor
of the horse-boxes. Heads appeared over the doors and
large soft brown eyes blinked at them curiously.

Felipe introduced the horses to her in turn, giving
them something from his pocket as he did so. They
whinneyed softly when he spoke to them, tossing their
long manes and snuggling their noses into his hand.
When they came to the big bay that Felipe usually
rode Julie caressed the velvet nose.

'They're all very beautiful,' she said.

Her surroundings rocked as he looked down at her
searchingly, and his white teeth flashed into a smile.

'I am pleased that you like horses. One day you must
ride with me. You will discover that it is much more
comfortable when sightseeing on the island.'

He had turned from his horse to give out the last titbit and dusted his hands with his usual fastidiousness,
and her heart played tricks at his nearness.

'Thank you for showing me your horses,' she said
formally.

'It is a pleasure,' he answered with a remote charm.

The housekeeper was waiting for them when they
returned to the house. Julie's clothes were dry and
ready for her to put on. Felipe drove her back to the
hotel and there was no sign of Roddy or his father

when they left the farm. There was little sign of the rain of the afternoon as everywhere had dried into a newly washed freshness.

Felipe insisted upon escorting her to the lift in the hotel, where he paused to look down on her gravely.

'Quite sure that you are fully recovered?' he asked, and again that charming smile appeared. 'I mean apart from the grazes on your hands. They will be very painful for a day or so.'

He was attracting several curious glances from guests in the foyer, but he was oblivious of them. Julie assured him she was feeling quite recovered as the doors of the lift slid open to receive her. She thanked him again and shot up to her room with a feeling of regret that the afternoon had ended so soon.

Roddy called her just before dinner that evening. He had returned the cycles and had settled for the damage to hers. He would not hear of her paying for it and he hoped she was not suffering too much from the accident.

She made light of it telling him that he was to think no more about it. Secretly, she would have gone through it all again to spend an afternoon with Felipe. Roddy was very disappointed at her insisting that they leave their next meeting to some date in the future, and she put down the receiver deep in thought. Was Roddy becoming too attached to her? Could it be the real reason why Felipe had asked her not to go out with him again?

Dale arrived to shatter her thoughts. Her skin glowed and again she marvelled at the change in her since she had come to the island.

'Have a nice day?' she asked, lifting finely pencilled eyebrows at the dressings on her hands. 'What happened?'

Julie told her and she gave a low whistle. 'Lucky it wasn't your face,' she commented. 'Who put the dressings on?'

'Felipe. I went to his place to get my clothes dried. Did you get very wet?'

Dale frowned, said quickly, 'What do you mean?'

'You were out riding, weren't you?'

Dale recovered herself and became wary. 'Yes, I was. I'd forgotten.'

'I haven't.' Julie leaned back against the edge of the dressing table and eyed her calmly. 'I saw you with José.'

Dale's lips thinned. Her eyes hardened. 'Have you been spying on me?'

'Of course not. We happened to be well above you in the hills.'

With what appeared to be an effort, Dale softened her expression and her voice.

'José goes riding with me sometimes. I'm lonely at times since Ricky can't get out and won't ride. He prefers golf in his leisure moments.'

She strolled to the window to raise her arms above her head.

'How I wish something exciting would happen!' she sighed, looking out over the grounds of the hotel. 'Do you ever feel like that?'

Julie said flippantly, 'Something exciting did happen to me this afternoon. I came off my bike and kissed the road.'

'I don't mean that kind of excitement,' Dale exclaimed impatiently. 'What do you think of Felipe? Handsome devil, isn't he?'

She swung round to look at Julie, whose face was suddenly suffused with colour.

'I thought you didn't like him,' Julie commented.

'I don't. But that doesn't mean I don't find him

attractive. I find José attractive too, in a different way. José smoulders in a kind of Marlon Brando way, morose but exciting.'

Julie said, 'I find nothing attractive in being surly and rude. I can't see why he attracts you so much.'

'José is a good friend to me.'

'Only a friend?' Julie queried meaningly.

'That's what I said. Make of it what you will.' Dale shrugged as if she could not have cared less for Julie's opinion. 'Are you coming down to dinner?'

Julie looked down at the small dressings on the palms of her hands. Her father would be sure to see them and she did not want him worried.

She said, 'I'd like a tray up here in my room if it's convenient. I'd appreciate it if you said nothing to Daddy about my accident on the bike. It isn't important anyway. If he asks about me you could say that I have had a hectic day and am having an early night.'

Julie felt a sense of relief when Dale had gone and she walked over to the window in the direction of the stables José rented from Felipe. Was that the reason Dale had gone across to the window to look for her friend? And why had Dale asked her about Felipe?

A lump came into her throat as she pictured him against the gleaming beauty of his horse. That was how she would always remember him, with those long sensitive brown fingers caressing the satin neck as he murmured gently to the horse, a heart-stirring picture of the beauty of form of both man and beast.

Softly through the open window came the strains of a guitar played by a master hand. The music came softly on the evening air. Julie sighed. It was impossible not to be moved by it; not to feel romantic in such idyllic surroundings.

If I could have two wishes at this moment, she thought wistfully, I would wish for Mummy and Daddy

to be together again and for Felipe to be as friendly
with me as he is with Sharon. How different it would
have been to have gone around his stables with her
hand tucked into the crook of his arm; to have listened
to his teasing with soft laughter on her lips.

CHAPTER SIX

AWAKENING the next morning was a painful business, Julie discovered. Her bruised knees felt stiff and her body was one big ache from the fall of the previous day. It was heaven to soak in the bath and to feel her body relaxing. The grazed cuts on her hands would heal quickly enough if exposed to the open air and there was only one cut on her right hand which really needed an adhesive dressing.

She put on a blue and white sun-dress, clipped white studs on her ears along with a choker of matching beads around her slim throat. A white chunky bracelet on her arm would take attention from her bruised hands and a swift brushing of the tawny hair completed a picture of youthful freshness.

She was stepping into her sandals when a tap came on her door and her father strode in, accompanied by Felipe.

Julie stared at them in bewilderment. Her father looked worried and Felipe was carrying a bouquet of yellow rosebuds with the dew still on them.

Her father wasted no time on preliminaries. 'What's this about you having an accident yesterday, and why wasn't I told?' he demanded grimly.

Julie refused to look at Felipe. 'Really, Daddy,' she said mildly, 'such a fuss over nothing! I had a spill, that was all.'

'Is that why Felipe came along this morning with flowers to enquire how you were?' He moved towards her. 'And what's this about grazed hands? Let me see them.'

Julie put out her left hand, which was not so badly grazed as her right.

'That's all it is.'

'I am sorry,' put in Felipe. 'I naturally thought that you had told your father all about it. Please accept my apologies for thrusting my presence upon you like this.'

'No need to apologise, Felipe. I appreciate your concern for this daughter of mine.'

'For you, Julie.' Felipe offered the flowers with a small bow. 'I trust they will help to erase an unpleasant incident from your memory. Such courage deserves rewarding. A Spanish *señorita* would have taken to her bed to recover.'

Julie accepted the flowers and breathed in their cool fragrance.

'Thank you, they're beautiful,' she said. 'Are they from your farm?'

'They were brought from Palma this morning. I ordered a bouquet for Doña Conchita also. I have just come from there.' Felipe's smile sharpened slightly. 'Doña Conchita was touched by your visit to a lonely invalid.'

Julie thought of José her nephew and Dale, but managed to smile.

'I hope she is well,' she said politely, and turned to her father. 'Dale took me to see Doña Conchita the other day.'

Her father smiled. 'How is her nephew doing in his latest venture, Felipe?' he asked. 'Dale seems to think he'll make a success of the riding school.'

Julie thought Felipe was too utterly at ease, his dark eyes too unwavering.

'Knowing José, it is too early to say. He has tried many things.' Felipe paused to look at Julie. 'Incidentally, my guests are out for the day—they have gone to see a bullfight. I wondered if you would care to come back with me to look over the house and farm?'

For one startling moment Julie found herself looking into dark eyes which inevitably captured her own. Her father's presence was forgotten. It was a dangerous moment during which she was inclined to follow her heart and accept his invitation. But it rang a warning bell.

Lowering her eyes to the flowers in her trembling hands, she said formally, 'Thank you for asking me, Felipe. I would love to come if I hadn't decided not to fulfil any social engagements until my hands are quite healed.'

Her father chuckled. 'But, Julie,' he remonstrated, 'you won't be expected to use your hands except for eating and drinking.'

Had she looked at Felipe Julie would have capitulated right away. To wander with him through spacious rooms, to gaze out on views familiar to him, was to have a glimpse of heaven. However, it would be more than foolish on her part to accompany him on a bittersweet tour of something that only dreams were made of. Dreams were dangerous, and with Felipe they were impossible. They were poles apart in their outlook and their upbringing. None knew that better than she.

She said, 'I'm sorry, Felipe. I was taking this opportunity of enjoying the amenities of the hotel for a day or so.'

Her father said in surprise, 'But, my dear, you can use the hotel at any time. Felipe is a busy man and might not have the time to show you around while you're here if you don't go now.'

'I know, Daddy, but I prefer to stay indoors today.'

'You do not feel well?'

Felipe was regarding her with some concern, and she gave him the briefest of glances.

'I'm perfectly well, and I thank you for your kind invitation. Some other time, perhaps?'

Felipe inclined his head and Julie knew that there would be no other time. Her father seemed lost for words. He was puzzled, she knew, as to why she had refused Felipe's invitation. The uncomfortable silence was broken by Dale bursting into the room.

'Felipe?' she cried on a breath of relief. 'I was told you were here. José would like a word with you.'

He raised a dark sardonic brow. 'Is José here?' he queried.

She nodded. 'He's waiting downstairs.'

Felipe frowned, none too pleased. 'It isn't bad news, I trust, about Doña Conchita. I have just come from there.'

'It concerns José,' Dale replied.

'Just a moment, Dale. I want a word with you.'

Julie watched her father leave the room after Felipe with his hand on Dale's arm, then she walked over to the window to gaze out towards Felipe's estate.

The day was suddenly meaningless, and once again she questioned her wisdom in coming to see her father. He had chosen to live his own life away from his family and she ought to have left it at that.

Her thoughts were interrupted by the telephone.

'Darling,' cried her mother, 'I'm in Spain—in Madrid on business. As I shall be there for a few days I wondered if you would like to come to spend next weekend with me. How is everything?'

By everything, Julie presumed her father was included.

'Daddy is well and everything is fine. What about you coming back here with me next weekend for a few days? Maybe then we could go home together?'

There was a pause during which Julie questioned the wisdom of such a suggestion. Her mother's presence could cause complications.

'We can talk it over when we meet,' was the guarded answer, and Julie heaved a sigh of relief.

She had her lunch in her room, then afterwards sat by the window with a book. It lay unopened in her lap as she thought about her mother in Madrid and began to understand why her father had chosen this lovely island to begin a new career. The temperature creating inertia could seep into one's bones like a drug. It could lull one into accepting the hand-outs of fate. Life in the hotel presented few problems provided one worked to enjoy it.

Inevitably her thoughts turned to Felipe. How heavenly it would have been to spend the day with him! There were going to be many more days when she would long to be with him, days which would lengthen into weeks and then years. Julie wondered if she could bear it, and in an effort to curb distressing thoughts, she opened her book.

Dale's sudden entry put an end to any concentration on the printed word.

She said baldly, 'I need your help, Julie. It's José! He's going to Seville to fight bulls, and all because Felipe won't loan him enough money to expand his stables.'

'Is that all?' Julie said mildly as she closed her book.

'All?' Dale echoed. 'Don't you realise that he could be killed?'

'So what?' Julie replied evenly. 'He's going of his own accord, isn't he?'

Dale eyed her in disgust. 'What about Doña Conchita, his aunt? It will break her heart. She relies upon him.'

'Are you sure that Doña Conchita's heart is the only one that will be affected? What about yours, Dale?'

'How can you talk like that?' Dale had worked herself up into a state of excitement leaving her pale and trembling.

By now the surprise of Dale's entry into the room had gone and Julie was the calm one. Common sense told her that Dale was not the kind of person to be so concerned about Doña Conchita. She was in love with José and was upset at the thought of him going away.

'What else am I to think?' she argued. 'You burst into my room to tell me that José is going away looking so upset.'

'Why shouldn't I be upset?' Dale broke in angrily. 'José is my friend. It isn't right for him to leave his aunt either when she needs him.'

'Has he told Doña Conchita that he intends to go away?'

'Yes.'

'And what did she say?'

Dale shrugged. 'You know some people. Too proud to say anything.'

Julie considered this, then said matter-of-factly, 'Is it possible that José is hoping that his aunt will give him the money he wants in order to keep him from going away?'

Dale was furious. 'That's a beastly thing to say! You don't know José or you wouldn't say such things.'

Julie said, 'Why so angry? And why is José so eager to expand his business so quickly? Couldn't he work it up gradually? He has no family ties and Doña Conchita has private means of her own, so he doesn't have to help her financially. There must be some reason why Felipe won't lend him the money. Maybe he isn't such a good investment.'

'And what exactly do you mean by that?' Dale snapped. She had gone pale beneath her tan and her eyes were hard. Julie was beginning to wish that she had gone with Felipe. At least she would have been spared this confrontation with Dale.

'It was the impression I had of him. In any case, I fail to see what I can do about it,' she said.

Dale put on a travesty of a smile. Her voice became soft, wheedling.

'You could go to see Felipe. Tell him that José needs the loan. He'll pay it back.'

Julie stared aghast. 'It's none of my business. How can I possibly go to Felipe and ask a favour for José? He won't take any notice of me. Why not ask Felipe yourself?'

Dale's expression remained sweet. 'I can't. He doesn't approve of me. You're Ricky's daughter, he'll do it for you.'

'It won't be for me. Besides, Felipe is the kind of man who doesn't change his mind when once he's made it up.'

'You can't be so mean as to refuse. Please, Julie!'

Julie stared as if she had not heard aright as Dale added,

'After all, we're giving you a good holiday.'

'You mean Daddy is. You have nothing to do with it. I'm his daughter.'

'And I'm here too,' she said loftily. 'I could easily have prevented him sending for you.'

'Oh no, you couldn't. Daddy has a mind of his own, which you'll have discovered by now,' Julie cried indignantly.

To her surprise Dale began to weep. 'You needn't be so beastly about it,' she gulped. 'I know I have no influence with Ricky, but I do want to help José. He's been so good to me. I had no friends here when we came and Ricky gave his whole time to the hotel. I would have gone mad if it hadn't been for José. I owe him a lot.'

Julie said impatiently, 'For goodness' sake, Dale, pull

yourself together. There's nothing to cry about. I can understand you wanting to help José, but I honestly can't see how I can help you.'

Dale dabbed her eyes with a wisp of a handkerchief. 'You can at least try. Felipe is on his own at the farm today. His guests are out.'

Julie consulted her wristwatch. 'But it's after three now. Felipe might not be at the farm when I get there. Besides, I have to change.'

'We can go now. I'll take you in the car.'

'What, like this?' Julie exclaimed, looking down at the sun-dress she had worn all day.

Dale glanced with approval at the long slim brown legs and soft white sandals.

'Why not? You always manage to look elegant in anything. I'm sure Felipe finds you very attractive.'

'Thanks. Flattery will get you nowhere. I'm not going,' Julie said determinedly.

Dale sat down on the bed, dropping her face in her hands. Julie ignored her. She was of the opinion that Dale was acting like a spoilt child and that it would be better for all concerned if José went away.

But it was not Julie's nature to ignore anyone in distress. With an irrational sense of disappointment over a day that had gone wrong from the beginning, she told Dale that she would go to see Felipe.

Before they were half way there, Julie regretted agreeing to go. She did not want to see Felipe. In going she was building up a heap of trouble for herself. If Dale was as attracted to José as she was to Felipe, then Julie felt sorry for her.

As they approached the estate, Dale stopped the car on a rise.

She said, 'We have a good view of the farm from here. It's possible we shall see Felipe on the estate.'

But there was no sign of Felipe. Their eyes combed

the vineyards, the almond orchards, the agricultural land, and Julie smiled with relief.

'He doesn't appear to be around,' she said. 'We'd better go back.'

But Dale was determined, having got so far. 'We can try the stables. He could be there.'

On reaching the entrance to the stables Dale stopped the car.

'I'll drop you off here,' she said.

'Aren't you coming with me?' Julie asked in surprise.

Dale shook her head. 'Better not. You'll do much better on your own.'

Julie met no one as she walked through the entrance to the stables, then her heart gave a lurch as she saw Felipe in a corner of the cobbled courtyard. He had evidently been out riding and he was bending down holding one of the big bay horse's legs to flick a stone from the hoof.

He had an audience of stable hands and his smile at them was white as he dusted his hands together. Julie watched him as, wide shoulders half turned her way, he patted the lovely arched neck before giving it a titbit from his pocket. He said something obviously in jest to his audience, who laughed as one of them went forward to take the horse's bridle.

When Felipe saw her he came striding forward with a look of astonishment on his face.

'Trouble?' he asked.

'Not really. Can I talk to you?'

He lifted dark brows and in the afternoon sun slanting across the cobbled courtyard his clear-cut features were very strikingly handsome. His narrow-hipped figure as he moved with an easy grace showed a quality of latent strength.

'Come to the house,' he said. 'You will pardon me if

I change my clothes. I have to rid myself of some of the grime I have collected while out riding.'

Julie walked beside him, determined to stop her capitulation to his charm. She had to stop caring for him. Once back home she would never see him again, she thought bleakly.

It was pleasant to enter the cool interior of the house where bars of sunlight filtered in between shutters to give the room a restful air. After seeing her seated in a comfortable chair, Felipe went to change. Julie closed her eyes. She had no idea what to say to him when he returned, and wished Dale far enough in getting her into such an embarrassing situation.

She opened her eyes as she heard someone enter the room. It was the housekeeper carrying refreshment on a covered tray. Her greeting was courteously polite, giving the impression that nothing Julie did would surprise her. The hooded lids over her dark eyes veiled a look that took in the long slim bare legs and crumpled dress. Then she placed the tray on a table near to Julie, gave her a polite smile and left the room.

Julie thought she was more or less prepared for Felipe's reappearance when he came, but she was not. He looked vibrant and glowing, his hair, black from a recent shower, was crisp and damply curling, and his smile rocked her heart.

'What is it you wish to see me about?' he asked, hitching immaculate linen trousers by their crease to sit behind the tray.

Julie watched as he poured chocolate into eggshell blue china cups and passed her one. His look was so quizzical that she came right to the point.

She said, 'Dale told me this afternoon that José is planning to leave the island because he wants money to finance his business.'

He smiled, said dryly, 'José has always been adept at

finding excuses for anything he does. You know he has approached me for a loan which I am not prepared to give him.'

Julie sipped her chocolate. 'What have you against him wanting to expand? After all, you rent him the stables. Surely it's in your interest if he wants to enlarge the business?'

'Not exactly. What José has in mind are more buildings in the region of the present stables, which means a spread over my land.'

'You can't spare the land?'

The dark eyebrows shot up, but his face was enigmatic.

'There is no point in discussing something that is over and done with. What is it to you that José has you as an emissary?'

He passed a plate of small pastries and she took one.

'Dale is so concerned because he will be leaving Doña Conchita when she needs him.'

'So Dale has enlisted your help on his behalf? Doña Conchita is not dependent upon José for anything except companionship, of which, in his case, she has little.'

'But he is a blood relation and Doña Conchita is dependent on visitors.'

'Not so much that José's absence would make much difference.' He drank from his cup and fixed her with dark eyes. 'What is your opinion of José? Do you find him attractive?'

She blushed, but not for the reason he would believe.

'I fail to see what that has to do with it?'

'I would say that it had plenty. Are you of the opinion that I should have financed José in this venture?' he shot at her.

She nibbled the last of her pastry. 'Well, you do rent him the stables.'

'So I do, but I have nothing to say on the matter except to repeat a warning I gave you once in respect of Dale. Leave well enough alone.'

Julie had the feeling that he had slapped her face, and she resented his high-handed attitude.

'You talk in riddles,' she said vexedly. 'I'm not interfering with Dale or anyone else. Dale has told me that José is a friend of hers and I believe her.'

'One thing you do not understand is the Spanish people. Take my advice and leave José and Dale alone.'

She stared at him in disbelief. 'All this because José asks you for a loan which you could very well give him?'

'Precisely,' he answered unperturbed. 'And now, if you will excuse me, I have matters to attend to.' He paused and his eyes narrowed. 'How did you arrive here? Not by cycle, I trust?'

He gave a half smile that did not reach his eyes. He was alluding, of course, to her bare legs and crumpled dress.

'Dale brought me. She's waiting for me at the gates. She's going to be very disappointed.'

He rose to his feet and said sardonically, 'That is life. We are all disappointed in life at some time or another.'

'Are you disappointed in me, Felipe?'

The words were spoken before she was aware of them and she blessed her ready tongue.

He lifted a brow in the attractive way he had and she was once more reminded of her not too immaculate appearance as he looked down at her.

'Why should I be disappointed in you? If you were a Spanish girl it would be a different matter. More chocolate?'

He bent down over the table to replenish her cup. She shook her head.

'In what way is it different?' she insisted.

He shrugged wide shoulders. 'Every race is different. Take Sharon. She is not like you at all.'

'But you like her?'

'Enormously. She is a well brought up young lady.'

'And her parents have not been divorced. Lucky Sharon!' Julie said tartly. 'Don't let me keep you. Sorry for wasting your time.'

She rose to her feet on trembling legs, blindly made her way out of the house and eventually found herself on the driveway. Angrily she told herself that she was a fool to come. But she had discovered that Felipe's feelings lay with Sharon. Well, Sharon was welcome to him! She would think no more about him.

Julie was a little out of breath on reaching the gates to stare with dismay to see that there was no sign of Dale or her car. She had gone. This is all I need, she thought despondently. There was nothing for it but to walk back to the hotel.

The air was still and very warm and she decided to go to the main road, hoping to get a bus. On the other hand she had a choice. There was a short cut back through Felipe's estate. Why not? She had all the time in the world.

She was wondering why Dale had gone when the big car slid to a standstill beside her. The front door of the car was opened and Felipe said, 'Please get in.'

Julie stood for several seconds staring at the dark unsmiling face. She was aware of her appearance as her clothes were already sticking to her warm skin. Her nose was shiny and she felt a mess.

'I am going to walk back,' she told him.

'You will enjoy the ride much better,' he replied firmly.

Julie made no move. In that moment, she hated him.

'I'm waiting,' he said patiently.

Silently she slipped into the car, slamming her door closed with more vigour than was needed in case he should lean across to ensure that it was closed firmly. Then she sat well back away from him.

Felipe set off at speed. 'It was commendable of you to come to see me on behalf of José. I appreciate it.'

Julie did not answer. Compliments from Felipe were just too much. She looked down at her hands and he noted the action.

'How are your hands?' he asked.

'Healing nicely, thank you.'

They were turning on to the main road and he glanced sideways at her averted profile.

'Why did you not accept my invitation to come to the farm this morning?'

'I wanted a quiet day at the hotel.'

'But you are here now?'

'I came on someone else's behalf. Dale was upset at the thought of José leaving the island. I didn't want to come because I knew I could do nothing.'

After a moment or so, he said quietly with a half smile,

'You tried.'

Neither of them spoke again and soon Felipe was slowing the car outside the hotel. By the entrance, he left his seat to help her out.

Coolly he said, 'I trust you'll have a quiet rest. Perhaps by tomorrow you will be feeling much better. Let Dale manage her own affairs—she is quite good at it, believe me. *Adios*, Julie.'

He was as distant as the snow-capped hills and as formidable.

'*Adios*, Felipe. Thanks for the lift,' she murmured, and went into the hotel without looking back.

Dale was on reception. 'How did it go?' she asked, looking up from a ledger on the desk.

'How did it go?' Julie echoed indignantly. 'You've got a nerve!'

Dale had the grace to blush. 'I left you to it because I knew Felipe would bring you back. After all, the longer you were with him the better the chance that he would change his mind.'

'Well, he didn't, and don't ask any favours of me like that ever again,' Julie said furiously.

Dale's mouth hardened. 'We haven't lost yet,' she retorted with an air of bravado. 'If José can't get the money from Felipe there are other places.'

'Just don't drag me into it, that's all. I don't see what all the urgency is about. Why can't José go on as he is until he can afford to expand?'

'He has his reasons.'

Julie looked at her sharply, wishing it was possible to probe beneath Dale's enigmatic look.

'Like going away with you?' she said in disgust.

Dale smiled tightly. Her tones dripped with honey. 'Now whatever put that idea in your head?'

Julie swung round on her heel and went to her room feeling anything but happy.

CHAPTER SEVEN

NEXT morning Julie caught an early bus into Palma. Her seat by the window gave interesting views of fertile plains where fig, lemon, and orange trees grew in splendid tropical profusion. Flowers were everywhere, hibiscus, oleander, and morning glory adding beauty to the enchanting country houses.

In the town she spent blissful hours admiring the handicrafts of the islanders, an exquisite variety of glass-blown objects in Gordiola, intricate ironwork in la Casa del Hierro, and hand-made leather goods in the shops along the Borné, where she had lunch.

After lunch a three-hour boat trip made her day. Seated on the upper deck of the white-painted craft, she sipped iced sangria and gazed spellbound on spectacular views. Towering cliffs swept down to narrow inlets fringed by shimmering sands, enchanting villas clung to slopes protected by sentinels of evergreens, and Julie soaked in the peace and beauty.

Her day was one of complete relaxation, and although no problems had been solved she felt the benefit away from them.

On her return to the Hotel Jacarandas, she was drawn immediately into a cosmopolitan atmosphere of leisure and luxury. The foyer was teeming with people who had come ashore to dine from the opulent yachts lying at anchor in the bay.

Her father with Dale was in the midst of it all, talking to three immaculately dressed Arabs in flowing white robes. Julie thought they looked remarkably handsome with their olive-skinned faces and dark eyes.

Crossing the foyer, she was aware of them all looking her way. One of them said something to her father
and the others took him up on it. Then her father
was frowning and shaking his head, which only seemed
to intrigue the Arabs more, and Dale looked on without
much interest as her father approached her looking
concerned.

He said quickly in an undertone, 'These Arabs want
to meet you. They're bowled over by your tawny hair
and white skin. They want you to dine with them, but
I told them that you had a fiancé who wouldn't like it.'

Leading her forward, he introduced her to the men
who were so mesmerised by her that Julie had to smile.
Laughter brought on by embarrassment bubbled in
her throat as she tried to control her mirth. The
Arabs, however, extended their hands as they
acknowledged the introduction.

Then her father was looking towards the hotel entrance at someone who had just arrived, and excusing himself, he strode towards him. After a hasty con-
sultation the two men joined them, and Julie found
herself staring up at Felipe as her father introduced
him as her fiancé.

The Arabs looked disappointed but not put out,
for they greeted Felipe with great friendliness. So
ludicrously embarrassing was the whole situation becoming that Julie longed for the sanctuary of the lift.

It was Felipe who eventually took the situation in
hand by taking a proprietorial grip of her arm and
leading her out into the grounds of the hotel.

'That was rather embarrassing,' she said with hot
cheeks.

Felipe released her arm to stare down at her with a
mocking smile.

'Those men are very rich.'

'But not in their experience of the Western world.

For instance, the colour of my hair might not have been natural.'

He surveyed the hair in question with greater puzzlement.

'You mean a wig?' he queried.

'No, no,' Julie laughed. 'I mean it might have been dyed that colour for all they knew. It isn't, of course, but I suppose they found it such a contrast to the dark hair of their womenfolk.'

Felipe was looking at her so intently that the colour again crept beneath her clear skin.

He said, 'Do you not fancy becoming the wife of a wealthy sheik?'

'I've never met any. I would imagine it would take a lot of adjusting to marry someone of another race,' she said frankly.

'It has been done,' he answered. 'I would say that you have the ability to adjust yourself to whatever you have a mind to. And love is a great leveller.'

A strange quality had crept into the deep voice and its gentleness startled her. He sounded almost humble. She was mistaken, of course. Either that or he had someone in mind when he spoke of love. Sharon perhaps?

'I suppose that's true,' she said lightly. Embarrassment made her voice sound almost flippant.

He had walked her on to the terrace and they stood looking over the balustrade towards the gardens and the sea.

'Have you ever been in love, Julie?'

He had turned to lean against the stonework and his dark eyes held her own captive. She thought quiveringly how incredibly dark they were, eyes which you could drown in. She blinked and broke the spell, shaken by the overwhelming wave of shyness washing over her.

'Lots of times,' she admitted after a slight hesitation. 'Adoration from afar, mostly. You know the kind I mean? Film stars, actors, celebrities—that kind of thing.'

She glanced at him briefly and felt impelled to joke about it.

'I've never been engaged before,' she added.

He looked startled for a moment, then he said gravely, 'Neither have I. Your father was concerned at the attention you were receiving from the Arabs. To invent a fiancé was the best solution.'

'I . . . see.' Julie could think of nothing more to say.

'You find the idea distasteful?'

'Not at all. Only it doesn't have to go any further, does it? I mean, I would hate to cause any trouble for you.'

'Trouble?' he said sharply. 'What kind of trouble?'

'Between you and any girl you have in mind at the moment. Some girl that you're fond of.' Julie was aware that she was babbling and that he was not amused. 'Or . . . or someone who's fond of you, like Sharon.'

'Sharon is one of my guests.'

Julie had the feeling of wallowing in quicksands.

'I know,' she said inanely. 'But you get on so well together.'

'Indeed we do,' he agreed, eyeing her shrewdly. 'However, I entertain a great deal, so I trust I am not expected to marry all my attractive female guests.'

'But you must find that some are more special than others, surely?' she persisted.

'That is so.' His white smile transformed the gravity of his dark features and she found herself drowning in his charm, as he added, 'Why are you in such a hurry to see me married?'

'I'm not,' she cried. Her voice wobbled, for they

were on dangerous ground. 'It's ... well, you're a very attractive man and a bachelor.'

Again he looked startled. The fact that he was unaware of his own good looks and charm endeared him to her still more.

She continued still babbling. 'I'm sorry, I shouldn't have talked about personal things. I don't usually do this kind of thing.'

She made a move to go, but somehow he was there barring her way. Maintaining that disturbing smile, he said audaciously,

'What kind of thing?'

Julie looked up at him, lost for words. 'You know ...' she began. Suddenly it was all too much for her and laughter bubbled in her eyes. Then he was laughing too and her heart skipped a beat as he bent his head.

'May I ask where you have been today?' he said politely.

'I've been to Palma around the shops, and went for a sail in the afternoon. It was glorious.'

She laughed at her own enthusiasm and found him intently studying her animated face. Her honey-tanned skin was flushed, her tawny hair a sunny halo around her enchanting face, and her eyes danced.

Felipe said, 'I am taking my guests to Porto Cristo to see the Cuevas del Drach. I take it you have not been there yet to see the caves?'

She shook her head. 'No, I haven't.'

'Then perhaps you will join us. Roddy intends asking you to come and the rest of my guests are very eager to go.'

'I'd love to go.' The words were out before Julie was aware of them. But she was in that kind of mood. She could not stop smiling and in that moment could not have refused Felipe anything.

'I will call for you at nine-thirty after breakfast.
Hasta mañana, Julie.'

Dinner that evening was a pleasant meal. Julie joined
her father and Dale in their private suite. Dale took
herself off after coffee and Julie went for a stroll in the
hotel grounds with her father.

She linked his arm affectionately. 'Why did you ask
Felipe to act as my fiancé earlier on?' she queried. 'It
was a little embarrassing.'

Her father took a long pull on his favourite cigar
and mulled this over.

'He happened to be there at the right moment,' he
said at length. 'I had to act quickly to put the amorous
Arabs off you once and for all. They were far too interested.'

She laughed. 'You know, Daddy,' she said lightly,
'it's funny you going all protective when I don't see
you in the length of a year.'

He said gravely, 'You're still my daughter and also
my responsibility since your mother isn't here. I don't
want you to marry the wrong person.'

'But, Daddy, I'm twenty-four. You aren't looking on
Felipe as a prospective son-in-law, are you?'

'Good heavens, no! The Spanish tend to marry their
own kind. Besides, there's plenty of time for you to
marry.'

Julie said frankly, 'I don't know that I want to
marry.'

She paused, then plunged. 'Daddy, Mummy is in
Spain.'

'In Spain?' he echoed, and gazed down at her in
astonishment.

She said offhandedly, 'She's in Madrid—something
to do with her job. She telephoned me to ask if I'd join
her at the weekend. I suggested her joining me here,

so the whole thing has been left in abeyance while we think about it.'

He was silent for so long that Julie had to speak. 'You don't mind her coming, do you, Daddy?'

The answer came in cool dry tones. 'Why should I? Your mother is a free agent and I don't own the island.'

'Nothing is settled,' she hastened to say. 'Let's sit down for a moment. It's such a beautiful evening.'

She gestured to a seat overlooking the sea and sat down to pat the place beside her. He sat down heavily beside her like an old man and leaned his arms along his thighs. The silver wings of hair at his temples looked more pronounced and he had a lost look which touched her heart.

'Would you say your mother is happy?' he asked, staring at the glowing end of the cigar in his hand.

Julie prevaricated, and laughed, knowing that she was near to tears and that she had to hide the fact from him.

'She leads a full life in her job, as you do with yours. Someone is always phoning her to ask her out for the evening. I don't think there's anyone special in her life yet, but one never knows whom she might meet up with on her travels. Mummy is a very attractive lady.'

'True,' he agreed, taking a pull of his cigar and staring out to sea. 'Is she bitter about the divorce?'

'Mummy could never be bitter about anything. She has a sweet nature. How do you feel?'

'Miserable and unhappy about the divorce, of course. I learned a great deal.' His smile her way was tight. 'You know, my dear, all men are selfish.'

Julie nodded in total agreement. 'Exactly what Mummy said. Mind you, she admitted there were faults on both sides.' She hastily changed the subject. 'What was Felipe doing here this evening?'

'He came to talk over some business.'

She said carefully, 'Did you know that José had approached him for a loan in order to extend the riding stables?'

'Dale told me. Felipe told me you were joining his party tomorrow on a visit to Porto Cristo and the Cuevas del Drach. You'll enjoy it. I was hoping that you and Dale would go about together. I haven't much time just now with the hotel.'

'One enjoys anything engineered by Felipe. I suppose he asked me to keep the number even. I can partner Roddy while he takes Sharon. She's very interested in him.'

'Who?' Her father seemed to emerge from a brown study, and Julie was sure he had not been listening.

'Felipe and Sharon, of course. I know she's keen on him, and he's going to the States at some future date.'

He sat up to place an arm along the back of the seat.

'Felipe is the type that girls get keen on. However, he refuses to be caught. I wouldn't say he won't marry eventually. But he's the kind of man who'll be master in his own household. He thinks, and quite rightly too, that a woman should choose a career or marriage. She can't have both. So take note, young lady,' he teased, tweaking a curl at her ear.

Julie was ready when Felipe called to pick her up the next morning. She was pleased with the hand-painted cotton skirt billowing out over a stiffened petticoat and the little sleeveless top with its tie boat neck in peasant style.

She had tied her hair into a ponytail for coolness and was looking for her capacious shoulder bag when Dale arrived.

'Is the hair-style for Roddy?' she enquired without rancour, as she sat on the bed to hug her knees. 'It certainly makes you look nearer his age. I came to ask you to work on Felipe regarding José. You know, drop a hint or two about Felipe being a public benefactor and all that. He gives a lot to charity and helps the island.'

'But not José. You never give up, do you, Dale? I suppose that's how you finally got Daddy.' Julie pulled herself up short on seeing Dale's expression change. 'Forget it,' she added. 'I don't want to quarrel. I'll think about it.'

She hoisted her shoulder bag, wishing it was possible to read Dale's thoughts. She had hoped that Dale would accept the matter of José as being closed. But it seemed she had not.

When Felipe arrived Sharon was sitting beside him in the big car. Roddy was in the back on his own. She learned later that his parents were spending the day with friends, having seen the caves at Porto Cristo on a previous visit.

'Hello, Roddy.' Julie greeted him in friendly fashion as he opened his door for her to slide in beside him. 'Nice to see you again.'

'Hello, beautiful,' he answered. 'What are you, a sprite of the morning?'

'Roddy, see that Julie's door is firmly closed. *Gracias.*'

Felipe spoke sharply from the front seat of the car. But Roddy did not appear to have heard him. He was staring at Julie with the kind of regard which worried her more than a little. Patiently, Felipe waited until Roddy got round to seeing that her door was firmly closed before he set the car in motion.

Felipe was annoyed and Julie wondered why. Was it her hair-style that he objected to? Surely he did not think that she was deliberately playing down to Roddy? Sharon murmured something complimentary about her peasant style blouse and they sped away.

Against the rotating windmills on the plains the sky was an eye-watering blue. There were fields of scarlet poppies and green vines on the way to Porto Cristo, which stood in a cluster of mellowed houses on the top of a hill far above the sea.

Julie loved the small seaside town with its inviting sandy beaches and white villas standing aloof on the high cliffs which formed the northern end of the bay.

The Cuevas del Drach, or Caves of the Dragon, were a short distance further on. Felipe bought the tickets to the caves and they joined a procession of people of all nationalities moving slowly down a steep narrow incline into the entrance.

To Julie's surprise the interior of the caves was warm and dry. So were the walls, the stalactites and stalagmites. The fantastic shapes of the petrified rocks were really beautiful and they must have shuffled down for about half a mile before coming to the Martel Lake, a vast area of clear placid water.

They now entered a chamber like a theatre with wooden seats set on a sloping dais on to which they all filed. The lights were lowered to the faint strains of music and three boats outlined in light came slowly across the lake. One of the boats had a small orchestra of four people and the music was magic, the spiral caves around them echoing the sound.

The air was humid and Julie longed to dive into the cool water of the lake. If only she could have experienced it with Felipe alone; to have been able to clasp his hand in moments of wonder and delight; to have been able to laugh up into his dark face and drown in the mocking gaze of his dark eyes. But at least she had seen it with him.

Gradually the lights came on again to reveal the beauty of a natural theatre with its endless columns of stone shining in an iridescent pearly glow.

They had to wait for their numbers to be called to be ferried across the lake again to the exit. The water was cool to the touch, salty and clear, and there was another steady climb after they had disembarked past the amazingly beautiful stalactites and stalagmites before they finally emerged into the brilliant sunshine.

The whole venture had been so meticulously planned and carried out that it all happened in less than two hours, and Felipe drove them to lunch at a hotel overlooking the delightful sandy beach and harbour of Porto Cristo.

Julie discovered that the joy of going out with Felipe was that everything went smoothly. There was no waiting for meals to be served, no second-rate service or food offered. He appeared to command respect and first-class service at the lift of one long finger.

They cruised slowly back, Felipe giving way to carts laden with brushwood which the islanders used for thatching. They stopped in Manacor to look at the cathedral, the spire of which was visible for miles among the greenery of the countryside.

Felipe explained that Manacor had been founded by the Romans and there were still traces of the time when they lived there. Coaches were parked in the cathedral square and the cathedral was filled with sightseers.

Julie wondered wistfully whether Felipe would get married in such a place and tried not to think about it as she found him by her side. He put a loose protective arm about her shoulders to keep her from being crushed by eager sightseers peeping at the many side chapels and pointed out the splendid baroque architecture.

'Are you enjoying your day?' he asked when for a moment they were hemmed into a corner by the crowds.

'Enormously. Thank you for bringing me.' Julie gave him a smile which was rather bemused. She had been savouring the peaceful atmosphere of the beautiful building and she did something on the spur of the moment which surprised even herself.

'If you'll excuse me for a moment there's something I would like to do,' she told him, and there in the small Lady Chapel she knelt down.

Her prayer was for her parents to come together again. Felipe waited for her, grabbing her elbow as she stumbled on going back to join him.

He said humorously, 'What did you pray for, a handsome husband with cash in the bank?'

Julie felt lighthearted and gay. 'I prayed for something that I want very much. It was something personal and I felt I just had to kneel down and pray.'

This time her smile was more pronounced and she tingled from head to toe at the grip of his hand on her arm. His well-shaped head was outlined against the beams of light from the windows, filling the lovely interior of the cathedral with light. Julie could not see his expression, but it did not matter. Everything was so unbelievably beautiful and soothing to the spirit.

He was looking down at her searchingly. The white lace scarf covering her tawny hair gave her an ethereal look that deepened the eloquent beauty of her eyes. She looked slender, youthful and very appealing.

The dark eyes narrowed more than usual and he said quietly,

'Is it trouble? Anything I can do to help?'

She shook her head so emphatically that his expression darkened.

'No, thanks all the same. There's nothing that you can do. It's sweet of you to offer.'

They seemed to have been trapped in the corner of the cathedral for ages, the place was so tightly packed with visitors. For Julie everything around her was blotted out. She was only conscious of Felipe looking down at her with the expression of a man who had been rebuffed. Bewilderedly she was asking herself why he should take umbrage at what she had said when Roddy bore down upon them.

'Where have you been?' he demanded. 'We've been looking all over for you. Sharon wants to go.'

Sharon had pushed her way through the crowd to link Felipe by the arm.

Poutingly, she said, 'I want a cool drink. All this sightseeing is completely exhausting.'

Felipe smiled down at her tolerantly. 'Then a cool drink it shall be, *niña*,' he said, and patted her hand on his arm.

They had their cool drinks on the terrace of a hotel overlooking the beach. When a vendor came round with souvenirs, Julie bought a windmill, the wooden kind that would remind her of the lovely drive to Porto Cristo and the caves.

For some reason which she could not explain she was finding it difficult to talk to Felipe or look at him. At the moment he was seated beside her staring out to sea. One long-fingered brown hand was curled around his glass on the small table. His clear-cut profile, so endearing, gave no hint of any thoughts going through his head. But Julie had the feeling that this trip to Porto Cristo was one he would be glad to put behind him when it was over.

On the return journey conversation was desultory as they sped through Felanitx and on to the rich agricultural land of Campos. They passed through a forest of almond trees and the ever-green vineyards turning to yellow in the sun, and saw black hogs instead of sheep in the fields.

At Lluchmayor they passed a busy market square

filled with local inhabitants enjoying themselves over
drinks in a delightful rural setting. Felipe explained
signs, buildings, monuments on the way in his charming deep voice and Julie gazed longingly at the back
of his head from her seat beside Roddy.

They were in the land of windmills when Roddy
asked Julie if she would go out with him the next day.
He had hired a car, a racer, low-slung and exactly the
thing for getting about. It sounded fun and she agreed,
partly because Felipe was becoming too important in
her life. She was deeply in love with him, nothing
could alter that, but she could endeavour to forget him
in Roddy's company.

It was only when Felipe was dropping her off at the
Hotel Jacarandas that Julie remembered with dismay
that she had not brought the subject of José up again
with Felipe. Bother Dale, she thought, it was none of
her business what José did. Or was it? Julie wished she
could believe that there was nothing between Dale and
José, for her father's sake.

She was relieved to see that Dale was not about, for
there was still an aura of magic in the air, a sense of
enchantment lingering on from her day out, and she
did not want to spoil it by talking to Dale.

Tomas was at the reception desk engaged on the
telephone and Julie saw him put it down as he saw
her to make a move her way as she went to the lift.

'*Señorita* ... Miss Julie!' he called, and she paused.
'A call came for you from Madrid while you were out.
Another call will come this evening. I will put it
through to you.'

'That's very kind of you, Tomas. I can take it in my
room when it comes.'

Julie gave him a warm smile and continued on her
way to the lift.

Mummy, she thought. I wonder what she's decided.

She was soon to know. Her mother telephoned as she was dressing for dinner.

'Hello, darling,' she said. 'Did you have a nice day? I was told you were out when I telephoned earlier.'

'Lovely. It really is a beautiful island. You should see it.'

'Maybe I will. I have a friend here who's visiting the island this weekend on business in his own private plane, and I might come with him. He has interests in the best hotels there, so I would have somewhere to stay at such short notice.'

'A friend?' Julie queried anxiously, quelling a sinking feeling in her tummy.

Her mother laughed softly, sensing her tension. 'Just an acquaintance, darling.'

Julie relaxed. 'That will be fine. Let me know the time of your plane and I'll meet you.'

Her father was not mentioned during the rest of the conversation and Julie put down the receiver with foreboding. Who was this man who was bringing her mother to the island? His name, her mother had said, was Frank Braddon, and he dealt in real estate. Julie sank down on to the bed to release her shaking legs from their burden. She was shattered.

It was not until that moment that she realised how much she had lived in the hope of her parents eventually coming together again. The very fact that her mother had shown no preference for any particular man among her friends had heightened that hope. Julie clasped her hands together as the moments ticked by, leaving her completely oblivious of her surroundings.

No one came to tell her that dinner was being served. Her father would probably have a tray sent to his office and Dale could be out. When Julie could not bear the dark thoughts running through her head any

longer, she rose, finished dressing, and went downstairs into the gardens. The thought of food choked
her.

She had enjoyed everything about the island, but it
was all underlain now with a flatness that hurt like a
pain. The enchanting evening, the whisper of elegant
gowns, perfumed and exquisite, as women arrived to
dine, the constant ebb and flow of talk which hitherto
had fallen on her ears so pleasurably meant nothing.

She walked slowly along the deserted terrace away
from the sound of diners from within the hotel and
pressed her hot forehead against the cool of a stone
pillar at the far end.

If she had spent her holiday with her mother as
planned this would not have happened. But it was too
late. She lifted her head as a nightingale began to sing
from somewhere in a tree nearby. The notes pouring
from its little throat were pure and sweet and so
poignantly beautiful as to bring the tears to her eyes. So
lost was Julie in the beauty of the moment that she was
not aware of the approaching figure until it joined
her.

Her breath caught in her throat as she turned to see
Felipe. Only he could be forgiven for breaking the enchantment.

'Hello, Felipe,' she said, blinking away the tears.
'Are you looking for Daddy?'

'No, you,' laconically. 'Shall we sit down?'

She sank on to one of the chairs on the terrace and
stared at his sober expression.

'It isn't bad news, is it?' she croaked in a hoarse
whisper. 'You look so serious. It isn't Daddy, is it?' she
insisted, recalling that she had not seen her father since
that morning.

He leaned back against the balustrade of the terrace
and looked at her for a long moment.

'It is Roddy,' he told her gravely. 'It appears that something was wrong with the car he had hired and he was putting it right for tomorrow. I believe he was taking you out with him for the day?'

She nodded. 'Do go on,' she urged.

'Apparently Roddy had put the car right and was taking it out on a trial run when he ran into a tree. He is lying semiconscious in a convent close to where the accident happened. He is delirious and keeps on saying your name. The doctor is of the opinion that the accident has been a lucky one. The concussion seems to be slight, but your presence is advised.'

Julie's reaction was one of shock. The blame was hers, because if Roddy had not been taking her out the following day he would not have been so eager to do the car himself in order for it to be ready in time.

Felipe was saying, 'You are not compelled to go, you comprehend? I made it clear to the doctor that you were nothing to each other. You are both young and Roddy is not yet out of his teens.'

He broke off to stare darkly at the tears welling in her eyes, and suddenly it was all too much for her. She wanted to put her head on his shoulder and wail. Instead she dropped her face in her hands and sobbed. She was hardly aware of the handkerchief he pushed into her hands, as it was some time before she could stop the flow of tears.

She found herself crying for Roddy. She was crying for her own stupidity in coming to the island in the first place. Not only had she fallen in love with a man who would be glad to see the back of her, she blamed herself for leaving her mother free to meet another man when she could have been at her lowest ebb, and now Roddy.

'Do you really care so much?' said Felipe as her sobs grew quieter.

Julie nodded her head, not bothering to explain that her tears were not all on account of Roddy.

'I see.'

Julie had sensed his sudden withdrawal and hastily dried her eyes.

'I'll come with you right away,' she said huskily. She gave him his handkerchief and rose to her feet.

'You need a wrap,' he said without expression.

She shook her head. 'Let's go.'

It was a bit of an anti-climax to see Sharon waiting for them in the front seat of Felipe's car. Her greeting to Julie was brief, almost curt, but all Julie could think about was Roddy. The convent was about twenty minutes away at the speed Felipe drove and they were soon entering a courtyard which suggested a cloistered silence.

The elderly nun who admitted them recognised Felipe immediately and motioned for them to follow her along a maze of corridors to one of the doors along a passage on the second floor.

When it opened at her knock she spoke softly to someone inside then bade them enter. Roddy lay on a bed in a small ward and as Julie moved forward he moved his head restlessly from side to side. His parents were standing at the other side of the bed and a nurse hovered by the window.

Dropping on her knees beside him, Julie took one of his limp hands and felt no response. Once in the dreadful stillness he muttered her name.

'Roddy,' she said earnestly. 'This is Julie holding your hand and talking to you.'

He made no response and she put his hand against her cheek. She went on talking and clasping his hand until her knees ached and her throat hurt. Roddy's family were talking in undertones with Felipe, but Julie never looked their way. Her tears fell on the

hand she was holding tightly in her own and gradually she felt it move.

Through a blur of tears she saw his eyes open as he
muttered her name. A few minutes later he was slipping
into a natural sleep. The nurse came forward and
helped Julie to her feet.

'Thank you for coming,' she said. 'He is sleeping
and will be all right now.'

Julie was in Felipe's car again, this time without
Sharon. She had not stayed long with Roddy's parents.
She could not forget that she had been able to do some-
thing for their son that they had been powerless to do.
She hoped they would not hold it against her.

Felipe had slipped out of his jacket as they left the
convent to drape it around her shoulders. Julie felt his
warmth seeping through her limbs. It was the nearest
she would ever get to him, she thought unhappily, as
she snuggled down into her seat beside him.

She glanced sideways at the wide shoulders in the
white silk shirt, the strong brown hands on the car
wheel and the clear-cut profile which told her nothing
of his thoughts.

He was the first to speak. 'How does it feel to bring
a young man back into normal being?' he asked dryly.

She said honestly, 'I felt awful. His parents must
have felt so helpless.'

'Not at all. Roddy is not seriously ill—he had slight
concussion. He will be as good as new in a few days'
time. I would not be surprised if he had been play-
acting a little in order to yet you there at his bedside.
It has been done before. You have been very good for
him. You have brought him out, given him the confidence he needed where young women are concerned.'

'I'm not arguing,' Julie replied, and hurriedly
changed the subject. 'Do you know a man named
Frank Braddon?'

There was a long pause during which she looked at him curiously.

Then he said, 'Why do you ask about this man? Do you know him?'

'No. He happens to be bringing Mummy to the island this weekend.'

He digested this in silence, then gave her a swift glance.

'You have sent for your mother? Surely your father is the one to ask for approval for your friendship with Roddy? Or has he told you that the boy is far too young for you to be serious about him?'

She said reasonably, 'No doubt both my parents would come to that conclusion, but they would never interfere with my life. They would certainly discuss it with me—but we're talking about Mummy, who happens to be in Madrid at the moment and who's coming to the island this weekend.'

His tones were coldly disapproving. 'Will your mother's visit not be embarrassing to your father?'

'I don't see why. After all, they are divorced.'

His smile was grim. 'I never cease to be amazed by the attitude you take towards divorce,' he said coldly.

Julie bit hard on her lip and did not attempt to hide her unhappiness.

'To be quite candid I was shattered by their divorce,' she confessed. 'Now this man is coming here with Mummy and I'm wondering if there's anything between them.'

'You would not want her to marry again?'

'No, I wouldn't.' She sighed and shrugged her shoulders helplessly. 'There's nothing I can do about it. I only want my parents to be happy.'

'And I presume that you want to be happy also. Are you in love with Roddy?'

Julie laughed. Even if Felipe was not interested in

her as a woman at least he was curious about Roddy.

'Of course I'm not in love with Roddy. Why, he's much too young. He's a nice boy, and I like him.'

Wryly he commented, 'At least we agree on that. Yet I have the feeling that his age would not prevent you from forming a lasting relationship with him if you were so minded.'

She frowned, wondering what he meant. 'Why should you say that?'

'You are unhappy about your parents. It upsets you to see them living apart, so what more simple than to marry someone who adores you in order to get away from an impossible situation?'

'You mean that Roddy offers an escape for me? I'll have to think about it,' she said flippantly.

He tossed her a grim look. 'I would consider it very carefully before taking such a step,' he said coldly.

The hotel was in sight and Julie was not sorry. Felipe appeared to be going hot and cold by turns, mostly his manner was disapproving, and she resented it. She had gone through a disturbing day and longed for the sanctuary of her room.

He was drawing up at the hotel when she bethought herself.

'You never said whether you knew Frank Braddon, did you?'

Felipe drew the car to a halt and turned to face her. The fading summer night filled the car with a muted glow which played on his lean clever face in a way that hardened his dark eyes. His mobile mouth was far from smiling and his finely cut nostrils distended slightly in distaste.

'Frank Braddon is a speculator of the worst kind. He is one of a number of such men who would ruin this island should they be given full rein. Your mother would be well advised to keep away from him and his kind.'

A little unnerved by his alien-sounding English, the cruel slant of his mouth, and his condemning tones, Julie retorted on a note of strain, 'I wasn't to know that and I'm sure Mummy doesn't know either. She ... she probably met him at the hotel where she is staying.'

Felipe did not soften. His voice still on ice, he said, 'I would say that your mother is like you in need of protection. I have yet to meet anyone more vulnerable. You certainly do not need a boy like Roddy for a husband. You need a man who stands no nonsense.'

Julie quivered inwardly. Her throat felt dry and she could not have been more distressed had he struck her. Anger followed the hurt, steadied her and pitched her voice on a low key.

'Thanks for the advice—I'm sure Mummy will be interested. Goodnight, Felipe.'

She stumbled from the car before he could leave his seat to open her door. Then she ran into the hotel without looking back. Phew, what a day! she thought. But it was not over.

Dale was evidently looking out for her arrival at the reception desk, for she hailed her as she crossed the foyer.

'Glad you're back,' she said crisply. 'I've been looking for you. Ricky isn't very well. He had a tight pain in his chest this afternoon just before tea, so I sent for the doctor, who told him to take it easy for a few days.'

Julie's heart lurched and she gripped the edge of the reception desk for support.

'Was it a slight heart attack?' she asked through pale lips.

'No. It could have been indigestion. The doctor

thinks so. He says Ricky has been doing too much. He has to relax and forget his problems.'

Julie drew in a deep breath of relief. 'Has Daddy got problems?'

Dale lifted her shoulders. 'Haven't we all?'

Julie wished she was more forthcoming and moved towards the lift.

Dale called after her, 'Ricky's in the room next door to his office. The doctor gave him a sleeping draught.'

Her father was asleep in bed. He looked boyish with the lines of strain wiped out in sleep from his face. Julie looked around the small bedroom with all the austerity of a man's domain and wondered why he had chosen to be in this small room instead of his own living quarters with Dale. She bent down to kiss his forehead, then quietly left the room.

CHAPTER EIGHT

As the morning progressed the tension Julie had felt on awakening that morning eased. Her father appeared to have recovered from his indisposition of the previous day, and was good-humoured and relaxed when Julie went to have breakfast with him in his office. He was obeying doctor's orders by resting in the small bedroom adjoining.

Julie knew that she was becoming hypersensitive about him, but she was worried about her mother's impending visit and how he would take it. She had arranged to have mid-morning coffee with Dale in their private suite and was on her way there when she saw Felipe striding along the corridor towards her.

She quivered. His skin had the healthy bronze of an outdoor life and he strode as if on a sweep of mountain air. In the well-fitting riding jacket his wide shoulders had a military smartness and he was so heartbreakingly dear.

He greeted her politely and after the usual preliminaries, asked, 'How is your father, and what exactly is the trouble?'

Julie regained her cool with an effort. 'Nothing serious, thank goodness. The doctor has ordered him to rest and take things easy. He's in his office and will be pleased to see you.' Lowering her eyes to the beauty of his well polished riding boots, she added, 'I haven't told him about Mummy coming. I'm waiting for a suitable moment.'

He gave a brief comprehending nod. 'I had no intention of saying anything of your mother's proposed visit. It is none of my business.'

His manner, while cordial, was studiously formal. He had come to see her father. He had no intention of improving upon this unexpected encounter with his daughter. But though their meeting had been abortive and impersonal in the extreme, she was still quivering when they parted, to carry with her the memory of his handsome dark face and enchanting deep voice.

How could she go away, she thought despairingly, when it meant leaving Felipe behind? The lounge of the private suite was empty when she walked in to see that a covered tray had been placed in readiness on a low table.

Restlessly, Julie wandered around the room wishing that the four walls would reveal the true situation between Dale and her father. It seemed so strange for him to be staying in the small office and the adjoining bedroom instead of the private suite.

'Sorry to keep you waiting.' Dale was there before Julie was aware of her. 'I see they've brought the coffee.'

Motioning Julie to a chair near to the low table, she served the coffee.

'Help yourself to sugar,' she said, passing a cup. 'That goes for the biscuits too.'

She sat down opposite to Julie, crossing long legs encased in green linen slacks, and sipped her coffee.

'Ricky says you've been in to see him,' she began chattily. 'He's much better, wouldn't you agree?'

Julie smiled tenderly. 'I'm happy that he's obeying doctor's orders. I don't think he's a hundred per cent fit, though. It isn't like him to be so docile.'

Dale shrugged and reached for an almond biscuit from a selection on a plate. Her small white teeth bit into it and she mulled this over.

'Now that all the excitement and hard work of

turning the hotel into a paying concern is over he might be feeling a little flat,' she said philosophically. 'He's put a lot into it.'

Julie's smooth youthful forehead creased into a frown.

'It's something Daddy has always wanted to do, and yet he isn't at all like a man who's realised his ambition. He should be elated at his success.'

Dale shrugged. 'I wouldn't know. Ricky never has confided in me.' She eyed Julie contemplatively over the rim of her coffee cup. 'Did you know Felipe is here? He heard about Ricky being ill.'

Julie blessed the sudden heat in her face and hastily lowered her head to her coffee cup in case Dale noticed.

'Attractive devil, isn't he?' Dale laughed, and dusted crumbs from her lap with enamelled fingertips. 'I've asked him to join us when he's seen Ricky.'

Julie stared at her in consternation. 'But why? I thought you didn't like him?'

Dale smiled. 'I still have hopes of him lending José the money he needs.'

Candidly Julie disagreed. 'You're wasting your time,' she told her confidently. 'For one thing, Felipe is dead against more building on his land.'

Dale's eyes were as hard as agates. 'Want to bet?'

For some reason or other Dale was in an exalted mood and Julie could hardly put it down to the fact that her father was not so ill after all. She wished futilely that there could have been more truth between them.

If Dale is expecting Felipe then I'm going, Julie thought firmly. She put down her empty coffee cup and dusted her dress with nervous hands for any biscuit crumbs prior to taking her leave. Then, murmuring that she had an important letter to write, she rose to her feet.

'You're not going yet, surely?' Dale looked offended. 'At least wait until I've fetched a fresh pot of coffee for Felipe,' she added in injured tones. 'If he comes and finds no one here, he won't stay.'

Julie hesitated, then sat down reluctantly. 'If you promise not to be long,' she said. 'You could ring for more coffee.'

Dale shook her head. 'This has to be special.'

Julie smiled. 'You aren't thinking of drugging him into submission, I hope?'

'It's an idea,' Dale replied, picking up the tray and making for the door.

For the next ten minutes Julie sat on the edge of her chair hoping that Dale would return before Felipe came. She was ready to go at the drop of a hat, so that when she heard a movement at the door she fled towards it to run into someone coming in. Strong fingers curled around her arms and a deep voice said mockingly,

'What a welcome!'

Julie raised her eyes no higher than the firm strong jaw. Untold fires sprang alight inside her at his nearness. She was aware of the faint aroma of good grooming, sandalwood soap and the tweedy scent of a good cigar.

'Sorry, Felipe,' she gasped on breath regained. 'I was just going to write a letter. Dale has gone for fresh coffee. She'll be here any moment—I'll go and hurry her up.'

His smile was openly mocking. 'Do you not want to know how Roddy is progressing?' he asked, still retaining his grip on her arms.

His eyes narrowed as he looked down at the clear eyes as colour crept beneath her creamy skin. The primrose and white sun-dress enhanced the colour of her tawny hair and she looked very young and vulnerable.

'Oh, goodness!' she cried. 'I'd forgotten all about Roddy in my anxiety over Daddy. What must you think of me?'

Felipe released one of her arms and kept a hold on the other while he led her back into the room.

'It is understandable,' he said evenly. 'You are upset about your father and rightly so. However, it gives me great pleasure to tell you that Roddy is much better. He sends you his love.'

He had closed the door and they stood looking at each other as he leaned with his back against it. Julie was at a loss for words and she longed to escape. Whatever was Dale doing? After all, she had invited Felipe, she thought angrily.

Remembering her manners, she was about to ask him to sit down when he strolled over to the window.

'I have some news for you,' he said quietly, and turned round to face her, leaving his face in the shade. She stared at his wide-shouldered outline.

He went on smoothly, 'I have found bigger stables for José with better prospects on the outskirts of Palma. It has splendid possibilities.'

Dale won't think much about that, Julie thought, then she remarked, 'Doña Conchita will miss him not being on hand.'

'José has never lived at Doña Conchita's house. He is at the moment living over the stables. Furthermore, his concern for his aunt has always been of secondary consideration, his first being mainly for himself.'

'Then if José is so selfish why are you bothering to help him?'

'José is a hard worker when he chooses to be. Lately he has not been so conscientious. Outside interests have diverted him.'

Like Dale, Julie thought unhappily. 'So you're re-moving him from the realms of temptation,' she mur-mured.

'Not exactly. He will still remain on the island, but it is up to him if he accepts.'

'Dale will be relieved. She was afraid he'd be hurt in such a dangerous job as bullfighting.'

He laughed at this. His teeth gleamed white in his dark face and her heart did a somersault.

'I very much doubt whether José would have carried out his threat to take up bullfighting to earn his money the hard way. He is given to flights of fancy from time to time. What he needs is a wife and family to think about.'

Julie considered this and said, 'I can't understand why Doña Conchita doesn't help him if he's her heir.'

'Doña Conchita is anxious for José to settle down and have a family.'

'Perhaps José doesn't want to marry. After all, you can't condemn him for doing something that you're doing yourself—remaining a bachelor. Perhaps he envies you your way of life—as a confirmed bachelor, I mean.'

Felipe was not amused. The very air bristled with coldness.

'I was not aware of being a confirmed bachelor,' he said frigidly. 'Who told you that?'

Julie was beginning to wish that Dale would put in an appearance, so ludicrously embarrassing was the situation becoming.

'No one,' she replied, moving across the room to grip the back of a chair in nervous fingers. The last thing she wanted to do was to sit down and have him towering above her. 'I assumed that you were.'

'I see.' His tones were as cold as an east wind and

she stared down at her fingers on the back of the chair.

The silence which followed provoked her to put her foot in it further.

'This place you have in mind for José—did the fact that it was some distance from here influence you in any way?' she asked.

He said bluntly, 'You mean in regard to his friendship with Dale? I am surprised that you condone it.'

'I don't. Daddy's duties at the hotel don't allow for much time to take Dale out. José is her friend.'

His voice was dangerously low. 'A Spanish woman would never dream of going out with a man other than her husband. It is not only in bad taste, it is asking for trouble.'

Julie felt she was fighting a losing battle and she babbled on more in self-defence than thinking of what she was saying.

'There is such a thing as platonic friendship in more liberated countries.'

'Nonsense! It is not surprising that your marriages go wrong.' He clicked his fingers disdainfully. 'One wonders what limits you place on social behaviour.'

Julie felt herself wilting beneath his anger. 'I'm sorry if you feel like that about us, Felipe.'

'I have never said that I do not like you.' Felipe had crossed the room to stand towering above her. 'You are misguided, but there is hope when you show this deep love for your parents.' A smile lifted the well-cut lips. 'There is even hope for Dale since she was concerned about José and his future. Does that surprise you?'

Julie did not answer. He was right in what he said and she wanted to tell him so, yet she could not without betraying her love for him. He looked thoroughly fed up and she felt a regretful pang at the way things had gone. She could not for the life of her look up to meet those smouldering dark eyes.

He was looking down on her tawny head, her eyes hidden from him by the fringe of lashes, and she looked young, defenceless.

Dale chose that moment to enter with a tray. 'Sorry if I kept you waiting, Felipe,' she said coyly.

But Felipe was already on his way to the door.

'Felipe!' Dale cried. 'You aren't going without your drink, surely?'

He paused at the door. 'I am afraid I must. *Adios*, Dale, Julie.'

Dale put down the tray as the door closed behind him.

'What's the matter with him?' She looked at Julie enquiringly. 'He looked as black as thunder. Have you two been quarrelling?'

'Where have you been, Dale?' Julie demanded. 'You left us alone deliberately, didn't you, thinking we'd talk about José?'

Dale smiled. 'No need to be mad. Many a girl would be delighted to be left alone with Felipe. What did he say?'

'Why not ask him?' Julie replied, and made for the door.

She ignored Dale as she called after her. She had suffered enough of Dale, José and Felipe. In desperation she thought of Roddy in surroundings which spelled peace. Leaving the hotel, she approached the taxi rank outside.

'Do you know the Convent of the Holy Child?' she asked the first cab driver.

She found Roddy much better. He was full of apologies for not being able to take her out. Julie stayed with him for about half an hour, then left, relieved that she had not seen the rest of his family. Roddy had to stay in bed for a few days.

She went on to Palma from the convent, strolled around the shops and had lunch. She spent the afternoon walking along the tree-shaded Borne where she sat with a cool drink at one of the many pavement cafés to watch the people go by.

She arrived back at the Hotel Jacarandas in the late afternoon and went right upstairs to see her father. He was in the office adjoining the small bedroom. He looked much better, but Julie thought he had lost his sparkle.

'Shouldn't you be resting, Daddy?' she asked, bending down to kiss him on the cheek.

He smiled. 'This kind of work won't hurt me, my dear,' he said. 'Enjoy your day?'

'Very much,' she replied, perching on his desk. 'Did you know Roddy had been in a car accident? I went to see him this morning. He expects to be out of hospital in a few days.'

He nodded. 'Felipe told me how you'd brought the boy round from delirium.' His look at her was searching. 'You aren't serious about him, are you?'

'No, I'm not. He's far too young. Felipe didn't say anything to you about him, did he?'

Julie put out a hand to touch the petals of a rose in a beautifully arranged bouquet of flowers set in a vase on the desk.

'No,' he said thoughtfully. 'That is, not exactly. He might have hinted about you and Roddy—I don't remember. The flowers are nice, aren't they? The hotel staff bought them.'

Julie smiled at him affectionately. 'Someone loves you,' she teased.

'They're a grand bunch and I'm lucky to get them,' he mused as though speaking to himself. 'Makes me wish I'd taken up this kind of work years ago. Things might have turned out differently.'

'Glad you like it.'

But Julie had her own reservations about realising whether his ambition had made him happy. The fixed smile he turned on her was simply not that of the father she knew.

She went to her room with mixed feelings. Dale said that she could think of nothing that was troubling him. Yet he was not happy about something. She had reached her room when she realised that she had forgotten to tell him about her mother coming that weekend. He had to know soon, but would it be wise to tell him right now.

She washed and dressed for dinner that evening, choosing a dress in leaf green. Simply cut in soft jersey, it went well with her tawny hair. With it she wore a gold chunky bracelet and matching ear-studs, presents her father had bought her for her twenty-first birthday. She was ready to go down to dinner when Dale flounced in. She was looking very attractive in shell pink with a high colour in her cheeks enhancing her prettiness. But it was the glow of anger. Every vestige of sweetness had gone from her expression leaving her eyes hard and bright. Her verbal attack on Julie was fiercely rendered.

'No wonder you didn't tell me this morning what you and Felipe have cooked up for José. Very clever of you,' she sneered, coming further into the room.

'For goodness' sake calm down,' Julie said quietly. 'I don't know what you're talking about.'

'As if you didn't know!' Dale snorted, shutting the door behind her. 'Pretending to be friends when all the time you were plotting with Felipe behind my back!'

'Plotting what? You know Felipe and I aren't close enough to plot anything. If you mean the stables he's offering to José, I had no part in that at all.'

'You might not have had a hand in the actual thing, but you could have dropped a hint or two about my friendship with José. I know Felipe doesn't approve of it and that the Spanish look on these things differently. It was easy, wasn't it, to persuade him to do something that would make José leave the district for another part of the island?'

Julie braced herself against her anger. 'I had nothing at all to do with it. I've never sought to influence Felipe in any way. You know as well as I do that Felipe is a law unto himself. He does what he pleases. You wanted José to be able to expand his business, so what are you so mad about?'

Dale's lips thinned. 'I won't have you interfering in my life! You've had it in for me ever since the divorce. You've tried to make something of my friendship with José and now you're trying to part us because you're jealous!'

Julie could only stare in amazement. 'Jealous of José I don't even like him. He's much too surly.'

'You're only saying that because he hasn't taken any notice of you!'

Julie said coldly, 'You're talking nonsense. Has he accepted the offer from Felipe? Is that why you're so angry?'

Dale's look was venomous. 'He hasn't made up his mind yet. I'm beginning to wish you'd never come to the island!'

Julie said calmly, 'That makes two of us. But don't worry, I'm only here for a holiday. The time will soon go.'

'It can't go too soon for me!'

With this parting shot Dale swung round and left the room, leaving Julie staring after her. She wondered how Dale would take the idea of her mother coming to join her. She would probably regard her as another enemy in the camp.

Julie dined with her father that evening in his office, and Dale was conspicuous by her absence. After dinner Julie persuaded her father to go for a short walk in the hotel grounds. It was a beautiful evening with a faint breeze coming from the sea. The nocturnal scents from the gardens mingled with the aroma of her father's cigar as they walked.

He said whimsically, 'You know, my dear, you should be out this evening with some nice young man instead of staying in with an old fogey like me. Why not go into the ballroom and dance? You won't have to wait long for a partner. The men will be leaving their womenfolk for you.'

Julie linked his arm affectionately and snuggled against him. 'You aren't an old fogey, you're only in your prime. Besides, I shan't be seeing you again for some time when my holiday is over.'

'That's true,' he admitted laconically.

They were silent for a few moments, then she said warily,

'What would you do if Mummy were to turn up unexpectedly?'

The words came slowly after a long pause. 'Is she thinking of doing so?'

'There's this man she knows who's coming to the island on business. She might come with him.'

'I see.' Another pause. 'Is he a special friend of hers?'

'I haven't a clue. If he is then I hope she comes with him. I'd like to look him over. Nothing but the best is good enough.'

'You're very fond of your mother, aren't you?'

'I love you both very much. I always shall.' Julie felt the lump in her throat growing into alarming proportions and she changed the subject. 'Where's Dale this evening?'

'Out with friends.'

She wanted to ask him if it bothered him who Dale went out with, but she had no right to interfere. She did not see Dale again that night and she went to bed thinking that no good seemed to be coming from her holiday with her father.

It seemed that Dale was avoiding her, as she did not see her the next morning. She had breakfast with her father again in his office and although he looked brighter he was not the man she used to know. She had bought a present for him when in Palma the previous day and one for Dale. It had been her intention to give Dale hers the previous evening, but had she done so Dale would only have accused her of buying her favours.

She gave her father his present at breakfast, a pair of hand-made leather house slippers. He was very pleased with them and Julie decided to give Dale hers later.

Tomas was at the reception desk when she went out later, but there was no sign of Dale. Julie spent a leisurely morning on the beach swimming, sunbathing and reading a paperback. Then she went to have lunch with her father in his office, but he had some business friends with him, so she went to the dining room.

Her morning on the beach had sharpened her appetite and she enjoyed the paella and the fresh salad with chicken. When the waiter brought her coffee he told her that her father wanted to see her in his office.

She found him surrounded by papers which he was gathering up to file away.

'Sit down, my dear,' he said, indicating a comfortable chair facing his desk. 'You didn't say what day your mother might arrive.'

Julie sat down to survey the back of his head as he filed the papers away in a cabinet. He had kept slim and fit, but his youthful appearance from the back did not match his face as he came back to take his seat at the desk and face her. She thought he looked tired and disenchanted with life.

She said carefully and truthfully, 'I've no idea what time Mummy is arriving. She said something about this weekend, which can mean Saturday or Sunday.'

He leaned back in his chair with a silver paper knife between his fingers and surveyed her soberly.

'I've given instructions for the room next to yours to be vacated by the weekend so your mother can stay with you.' He broke off to raise a brow at her change of expression. 'You don't appear to be overjoyed at the thought?'

She moistened dry lips and tried to explain. 'Mummy may not want to stay here at the hotel. I'm sure Dale wouldn't like it either.'

He said grimly, 'Dale won't care one way or the other. Don't you want your mother to stay here with you?'

'You're forgetting something, Daddy. The man who's coming with her has interests in hotels here and it's possible that he's arranged for her to stay in one of them as his guest.'

His jaw tightened. 'Then we shall have to wait and see. How are you and Dale getting on?'

'As well as can be expected,' she replied, putting on a carefree attitude. 'Where is she, by the way? I haven't seen her.'

He gave a wry smile. 'Dale pleases herself where she goes and what she does, more or less.'

Julie managed what she hoped was a smile. She had a feeling that her father was going to be hurt and there was nothing she could do about it.

'How are you feeling?' she asked by way of changing the conversation.

He appeared to be in a brown study and she repeated her question.

'Sorry,' he said. 'You know, it's really uncanny, your voice, the way you smile gave me quite a turn. Strange how I've never noticed it before, this likeness to your mother.'

Julie shrugged. 'There's a saying that we only see what we want to see.'

Her father rose to his feet and made for the drinks cabinet.

'Like a drink?' he asked.

She shook her head. 'Too soon after lunch, and I don't drink. You used not to either.'

He laughed and she heard the clink of a bottle touching glass. She turned to see him leaning against the cabinet with a jaded smile as he sipped the golden liquid in his glass.

'People change, my dear, or rather circumstances change them. Your mother used not to drink much either. Has she changed?'

'That would be telling, wouldn't it? A lot of people drink because they're unhappy.'

'Is your mother unhappy?'

Julie frowned. 'What is this, Daddy, an inquisition? For your information, Mummy looks younger than ever, dresses beautifully and fills every minute of her day.'

She rose to her feet feeling near to tears. As usual she had said far too much, even if everything she had told him about her mother was true. What she had not told him was that, in her opinion, all her mother's actions were deliberate, giving the impression that she was driving some fast and powerful car against all comers.

Her father tossed off the rest of his drink. Was it wishful thinking on her part or had the conversation touched some sensitive spot? Did he still love her mother? He looked a little pale around the mouth, but that could be due to strain from doing too much, or worrying about Dale. Was he afraid of losing her? She longed to ask him what was really troubling him. Instead she said,

'It's far too nice to stay indoors. How about going to the hotel swimming pool with me?'

'Not today. You go and make the best of your holiday.' He smiled fondly at her putting an arm around her shoulders as she rose to her feet. 'You have quite a nice tan and it becomes you.'

'You're losing yours,' she replied forthrightly. 'And you know you've been advised to take things easy.'

He shrugged. 'I wouldn't be very bright company just now. Run along and enjoy yourself.'

She tiptoed to kiss his cheek. 'Be seeing you. Take care of yourself!'

She was on the way to her room when she heard the click of a door along the corridor in the direction of her father's private suite. Normally, not being the inquisitive type, she would not have given it a second thought, but some sixth sense alerted her and she slipped hastily into her own room to wait with door slightly ajar.

It came as something of a shock to see Dale go by carrying a suitcase. She had already gone into the lift before Julie could summon any action in her limbs. There was only one thing to do—bring her back. Her father was in no fit state for shocks.

Instantly the thought of José and his aunt Doña Conchita came to mind. Doña Conchita would know if José had gone away.

Hurriedly changing into one of her prettiest summer

dresses, a white glazed cotton with sprays of lavender
giving it a cool crisp appearance, Julie trod into white
sandals and recalled two bottles of eau-de-cologne
which she had bought the previous day. One was for
Dale and the other for her mother, but she could buy
another for her mother. Doña Conchita would find the
eau-de-cologne deliciously cool and soothing in the
heat of the day.

The maid let her into the house and took her to
Doña Conchita's room without delay. Julie had the
confined feeling of a sudden oppression on going from
the bright warm sunlight into the gloom of the shady
interior. But Doña Conchita's room was bright with
flowers and her sallow face showed soft colour.

She was obviously pleased to see her and shyly
accepted the cologne in her gracious way. The maid
was sent to bring chocolate and refreshments and Julie
was thankful that Doña Conchita could speak excellent
English. They drank chocolate, nibbled pastries and
talked, while Julie strained her ears for José who
might be calling in to see his aunt.

Doña Conchita asked her how she liked the island
and told her of walks she would enjoy. There was no
mention of José and Julie was beginning to wonder
how on earth she could broach the subject when there
was the sound of someone arriving. Doña Conchita
lifted her head to listen in the manner of one expecting a caller, and in strode Felipe.

Doña Conchita's face was rosy with pleasure. 'We
have a visitor, Felipe, and a very charming one.'

'So, I come with flowers to cheer you, only to find
that someone has beaten me to it.'

Felipe came forward after placing a gift of flowers
on a chair to greet Doña Conchita. Her bird-like glance
followed his to the pretty bottle of eau-de-cologne
which Julie had brought.

She said with pleasure, 'A present from our little English visitor. It is my lucky day, to have two beautiful presents brought by beautiful people.'

In her pleasure, she looked much younger and very mischievous. With a coquettish glance at Felipe's dark lean face, she added, 'Would you not agree, Felipe, that our Miss Julie is like a flower herself?'

Felipe's white smile flashed and the near-black eyes were directed upon Julie, upon her fair tanned skin, the lovely eyes tilting slightly at the corners and the tawny hair falling naturally into silky abandon.

With a tinge of colour in her cheeks Julie tried to ignore that white smile, a most infuriating attribute in her opinion of a most infuriating man. But Felipe was his usual cool self and he replied in slow measured tones.

'A rather delicate bloom from a cool English garden come to brighten our dull lives for a short time. We shall be all the poorer for her going.'

He glanced from Julie's embarrassment to Doña Conchita's sweet face and began a conversation entirely for Doña Conchita's benefit. At her request he fetched a deed box from a nearby desk and took out some papers which they perused between them.

Doña Conchita's attention to detail was sharp and concise. They spoke for ten minutes or so on matters which held no interest to Julie since they conversed in Spanish. Then the box was returned to the desk and Doña Conchita had an expression of satisfaction on her face.

Julie wondered what they were cooking up between them, in between wondering what had happened to Dale and José. Since José had not appeared she was surmising that he and Dale could have gone away together. She had to know if it was true, and Felipe would tell her. She could trust him to find out for her.

Felipe refused chocolate and soon Doña Conchita's eyelids began to close in her usual afternoon nap. It was then that he rose to his feet to offer Julie a lift back to the hotel.

'I'd like to talk to you if I may,' she said as they made their way to his car.

'Would you prefer a stroll along the beach?' he asked. 'The car will be like an oven inside from the sun.'

The tide had recently gone out and they walked along the hot sand already drying in the sun. The tang of wet seaweed mingling with the salty breeze coming from the sea was heady—or was it Felipe's nearness?

'You wished to talk to me?'

His tone was cool and impersonal, and Julie hesitated.

Was it wise to involve him in family matters? she asked herself. He had already advised her not to interfere in Dale's affairs. But this time her father's health was at stake. Besides, Doña Conchita was involved too. She would be upset if her nephew had gone away with Dale.

He prompted her as if aware of her indecision. 'Is it your father?' he asked.

She told him of her fears, of seeing Dale with a suitcase leaving the hotel earlier that afternoon.

'I'm worried about the effect it will have on Daddy,' she went on. 'He isn't well enough to have a sudden shock.'

There was a brief silence, then Felipe spoke evenly and without surprise.

'Why do you think that Dale has gone away with José? Did she leave a note?'

'I don't know.'

'Did you ask Doña Conchita if José had gone away? I presume that was the reason for your visit to her.'

Julie felt the colour staining her cheeks. These dark eyes of his never missed a trick. She felt small and mean and angry because he made her feel so.

'I never said anything to Doña Conchita, nor was I intending to. I did hope I would hear something to the effect that José had gone away, but I had no intention of upsetting the Señora,' she said indignantly.

'I never for one moment thought that you had or would do, Julie. I think we had better see José to find out what is going on.'

His tone, his whole manner had softened to such an extent that Julie looked up at him startled. In doing so she caught her ankle on a rock jutting out of the sand and for seconds the pain made her feel sick as she crumpled on the ground.

Suddenly he was bending over her with concern. 'What happened?' he asked holding out a hand to help her up.

She sat up on one bent leg with the injured ankle stretched out on the sand. Julie tried not to look at him as the pain lessened—or had it moved to her heart? She wanted Felipe so much, but was wanting enough? She wanted her parents to be united and she wanted Felipe. Was she being too selfish in wanting the two things that made life worth living?

Felipe had taken her sandal off. 'Can you move your toes at all?' he asked, gently moving his fingers around her ankle.

Julie could move her toes easily enough. The ankle was bruised, but no real harm had been done.

'It doesn't hurt much now,' she told him. 'I'd like to try to stand on my foot. Please,' she begged as he hesitated.

His regard was narrow-eyed as he ignored her plea. Lifting her beneath her arms on to her good ankle, he picked her up in his arms with ease and carried her back to the car.

When she was in her seat he took his place behind the wheel. 'I had better take you back to the hotel. It would be wise to let the doctor see your ankle.'

'But we were going to see José,' she protested.

'This is more important.'

Julie said desperately, 'Please let's go to find José! I must know because of Daddy. If Dale has gone away with him Daddy will have to be told.'

Felipe started the car and they left the village behind. It was not long before they were on the estate, threading their way between vineyards and almond orchards to the stables. Julie's ankle still ached, but the pain was nothing compared with her anxiety about her father. Then Felipe was speaking.

'How do you feel about the possibility of Dale going away with José? Does it make you happy?'

Julie bit hard on her lip. Quietly and quaveringly she said,

'I want Daddy to be happy. I know he isn't at the moment. Maybe he's worrying about Dale—I don't know.'

Tears sprang to her eyes and to her mortification Felipe glanced at her before she could blink them away.

He said crisply, 'You are meeting trouble half way. You might be in for a surprise. How well did you know Dale before she went away with your father?'

'Well enough. She was my friend.'

'And did you share her sentiments?'

'We weren't very much alike, if that's what you mean. Dale was rather mercenary, always talking of marrying for money. It was a kind of obsession with her. That was why I was so surprised when she went after Daddy.'

'So you are not in her confidence. You are taking it

for granted that she is in love with José?'

'What else am I to think when she goes hysterical because he might go away?'

He said dryly, 'Not so long ago you mentioned something about platonic friendship between them.'

Julie gave him a sideways glance. His clear-cut profile was unyielding. He seemed to have withdrawn into himself and was taking sides against her. She knew how proud, generous and devout the Spanish people were and that they could be even a trifle narrow-minded in their simplicity. But she had taken it for granted that Felipe, well educated, experienced, would appreciate what she meant by platonic friendship.

'Familiarity breeds contempt,' she scoffed. 'Is that how you regard a woman's friendship with a man in Spain?'

He said coldly, 'We prefer our women to be virgins until they marry. That way we believe their children will be healthy.'

They were approaching the stable and Julie looked round hopefully for José. The car slid silently into the courtyard, Felipe braked and for a moment or so they sat in silence.

He was looking down at her legs. 'How is the ankle?' he asked.

Julie gave a start, having forgotten all about it. The swelling had not gotten worse and she wiggled her toes in her sandals.

'Not bad at all, thanks,' she replied.

'All the same, it could need medical attention.'

Felipe got out of the car and walked across the courtyard, with that easy grace that was so much part of his charm. The proud set of his well-shaped head, the wide shoulders carried so arrogantly with a military smartness sent emotions crowding in on her alarmingly. Filled as she was with emotions already tearing her apart, such feelings were dangerous.

Her need of him blacked out all other things. She
wanted to tell him how much she loved him, that she
would be everything he asked of a woman, but he regarded her as misguided, frivolous, and a possibly
promiscuous person, when she was so very much different.

Julie's throat felt blocked with emotion. She wondered what his wife would be like when he married.
Somehow she knew it would not be Sharon. A Spanish girl with melting brown eyes, seductively demure
with hair black as a raven's wing, someone who had
the look of one who had been reared on peaches and
grapes?'

She drew in a long breath and watched him go
into José's office. Within seconds he was out again,
dropping easily down the steps and making his way to
the stables. When he reappeared some time later, Julie
knew he had not found José. His smile as he returned
to the car was meant to banish her expression of anxiety.

'José has gone out,' he said reassuringly. 'I suggest
we return to the hotel to see if Dale is there. She
could have been using the case to carry something to
someone.'

Julie looked directly into his dark eyes. 'You don't
think that, do you?' she said with wide-eyed apprehension.

He smiled again, a strange sort of smile, then set the
car in motion.

'First we will call on the doctor on our way to the
hotel for him to examine your ankle. We shall then
continue on our way to the hotel.'

'The hotel, please, Felipe. We must make sure about
Dale. My ankle doesn't bother me, and the swelling
is going.'

Julie looked at him appealingly, but he had his eyes on the road ahead.

'If we go to the hotel first,' he said at last, 'you will remain in the car while I make enquiries.'

Dale was not in the hotel, Felipe assured her after ten minutes spent inside making discreet enquiries. Julie went pale as he slid into the car beside her to impart the news.

'Did you see Daddy?' she asked weakly.

'No, I did not.'

Julie looked at him helplessly. 'Oh, Felipe!' she cried, fighting back the tears. 'What shall we do?'

'First of all you have to stop upsetting yourself over something you cannot help. Secondly, you will now step out of the car and show me if you can walk with your injured leg.'

He went round to her door to help her out, retaining a hand on her arm as she straightened to stand on her feet. Gingerly she walked a few steps, then smiled up at him triumphantly.

'Perfectly all right. A bit sore, that's all.'

'Good.' His smile rocked her heart. 'And now we will go to my farm for your English tea. I have something to tell you.'

His hand was still on her arm and Julie lowered her eyes, in danger of betraying her love for him. Then, as she hesitated, a big car drew up behind Felipe's and she was greeted by a familiar voice.

'Julie!' Her mother, a vision in powder blue and looking, Julie thought tenderly, younger than ever, was out of the car and rushing towards her.

Julie gurgled with delight as she kissed her.

'So this is Julie!'

A man had slid from the car and Julie disliked him on sight. There was no reason why she should behave so irrationally. There was nothing offensive about him.

His clothes were expensive and immaculate, his hair had been styled by an expert and he was rather good-looking. His age, which Julie guessed was around forty, was accentuated by the white wings of hair at his temples. But he was too suave, too calculating in his appraisal of herself.

A slight shiver ran through her as she met his pale grey eyes and she turned instinctively to Felipe just in time to see his car sliding away.

Her mother was saying, 'Yes, this is my beautiful daughter. Julie, I want you to meet Frank Braddon, who was kind enough to bring me here and fix me up in a lovely hotel.'

Julie felt that it was one of the worst moments of her life. This Frank person had arranged for her mother to be in daily contact with him at one of his hotels, and she shuddered to think what the outcome might be.

Julie had never given a thought to her mother marrying again. Yet her common sense ought to have alerted her to the possibility of it. Anyone as attractive and sweet would not be without admirers who would want to marry her.

Julie murmured the conventional greeting before speaking again to her mother. They both began to speak together and ended up laughing.

Her mother spoke first.

'We want you to have tea with us at the hotel where we're staying.'

'But Mummy,' Julie cried, 'this is the hotel Daddy is managing. The Jacarandas. Isn't it beautiful?'

Frank Braddon surveyed the lovely façade of first-rate Spanish architecture with a supercilious smile.

He said gruffly, 'I have some business to attend to, so why don't you two have tea together? Julie can dine with us this evening.'

Julie seized on the suggestion eagerly. 'Let's have tea here on the terrace, Mummy,' she cried. 'Dale is out and Daddy is upstairs in his office.'

Her mother was reluctant. 'On one condition—that you don't tell anyone here who I am. I want no complications.'

They found a corner table at the end of the terrace and Jaime came to serve them.

'Tea for two, Jaime, please, with some of those delicious pastries,' she said with a fond smile.

When he had gone, her mother said, 'I have to watch my weight since I came to Spain. I love to sample everything that's going, and that's bad. Now tell me what you've been up to. Does your father know I'm coming?'

Julie nodded, noticing the colour creeping under her mother's clear skin as it did at the mention of her father.

'Actually we were expecting you this weekend, and as today is Friday you've caught us out. Daddy has a room for you next to mine, but it won't be vacant until tomorrow.'

Her mother took off her gloves and smiled. 'Then that lets me out of staying here,' she said lightly with obvious relief. 'Who was that perfectly lovely young man you were with just now?'

Julie laughed as Jaime arrived with their order.

'Felipe,' she answered when Jaime had gone. 'He's a farmer, among other things.'

She felt her colour rise at mentioning Felipe, but her mother was pouring out the tea.

'Mummy,' she asked to cover her own embarrassment, 'how serious are you about this Frank person?'

'Darling, don't be so crude! The man has a name. He's been very kind to me and I want you to look upon him as a friend also.'

Julie met the fond smile and accepted the cup of tea. Her heart dropped as her worst fears seemed to be materialising, sending a dark cloud over the brightness of her day. Her fingers tightened on her cup which she lowered to the table with unsteady movements.

Baldly, she said, 'Daddy isn't well. The doctor says he has to take things easy.'

Her mother held a pastry in mid-air and went pale. 'But you said he was working in his office?'

'So he is. He has a bedroom adjoining it that he's using at the moment. I suppose he finds it more convenient than moving all his office files to his private suite.'

'I see.' Her mother put down the pastry and took a drink. 'And where is Dale?'

'Out at the moment,' Julie said matter-of-factly after deciding to say nothing more until she had seen Felipe again.

'What exactly is wrong with your father?' her mother asked. 'He's always been as strong as an ox—never had a day's illness in his life that I can recall. The last thing I would have associated with him would be a dicky heart.'

Julie smiled brightly, hating to see her mother look so unhappy.

'I don't think he has a weak heart or anything like that. In my opinion he's been driving himself too hard, like you. Now that he's achieved his objective in making a success of hotel management, he's feeling let down with much less to do.'

Her mother looked militant. 'Why should you say I've been driving myself too hard?'

Julie stuck to her guns. 'You have, Mummy—you know you have. Ever since the divorce you've been here, there, and everywhere.'

'What did you expect me to do, fall flat on my face

and feel sorry for myself?' her mother cried indignantly. 'I'm happy in my work. Will you believe that?'

Julie shook her head sadly. 'I'd believe you more if you didn't glare at me as you're doing now. When you're happy it shows. I'm not happy—but I'm not going to marry the first likeable man I meet either to escape that unhappiness.'

Her mother's blue eyes hardened with anger. 'If that's a dig at me regarding Frank all I can say is— mind your own business!' With trembling hands she picked up her handbag and gloves, threw some money on the table to pay for the tea, and said, 'Maybe you'll be in a better mood this evening when we call for you. Goodbye, Julie.'

The next moment she had gone, leaving Julie sitting alone staring at her empty chair. There had been little friction between them through the years and to reach an impasse like this was shattering, Julie thought in despair. It was some time before she left the table to make her way into the hotel.

A peep in her father's office revealed him sleeping in his chair at his desk with an afternoon tea tray at his elbow. Maybe she would have news of Dale later when she told him of her mother's arrival on the island.

She washed and changed early that evening and went to the private suite in case Dale had returned. There was no answer to her knock.

Back in her room she telephoned Felipe to ask of news of Dale, to find that he was not in. There was nothing for it, she told herself, but to tell her father of her mother's arrival.

She telephoned his room to spare him any embarrassment he might show on learning about his former wife. She told him that her mother had booked in at the hotel of her friend and that she was dining with her that evening.

He took the news quietly, said she was in good hands and wished her a nice evening. No, he had no message for her mother. He had not seen Dale either, he said in answer to her query, which was not surprising since she was not on duty at the reception all day. She was taking the day off.

Julie sighed with exasperation, put down the telephone and went in search of Tomas to see what she could get out of him concerning Dale. But Tomas was not on reception and she decided to take a short walk in the gardens until he returned.

The diners had not yet begun to arrive and with most of the hotel guests dressing for dinner, Julie had the gardens to herself. She had walked the length of the terrace when she turned to look back and saw ... Felipe.

He came striding towards her and she braced herself against his charm.

'I saw you as I was driving to the hotel entrance. The terrace is visible from the road,' he said without preliminaries. 'How is the ankle?'

'Not too bad. I was just thinking about you.'

The dark silky eyebrows shot up in surprise. 'I trust that they were kind thoughts,' he murmured. 'Shall we sit down? I have news for you.'

He led her by the elbow down the steps of the terrace and on to a garden seat beneath the balustrade. He was wearing a smart city-going suit and he looked tanned and vital. Julie sank weakly into one corner, leaving him to take the other. The space between them enabled her to study his profile as he stared out at the garden.

'I have seen José,' he began. 'You were only half right when you surmised that Dale had run away.'

Eagerly, she said, 'You mean José has brought Dale back?'

'On the contrary. José took Dale to meet the person with whom she was having an affair,' he informed her dryly.

Julie lifted her hands to burning cheeks. 'Oh dear! You mean there is someone else ... that Dale has run away with a man after all?'

He turned his dark disturbing eyes upon her. 'This will come as a surprise to you, but Dale was never in love with José, neither did she have an affair with him. José was merely the go between for her and her lover, a man named Gerald Euston.'

'Euston?' she echoed. 'Isn't he the millionaire race-horse owner?'

'He has a yacht out in the bay here ... or had. He has gone, taking Dale with him. They are going to be married—later, of course. José trained several of his horses and Dale met him at the stables where José introduced them. The attraction between them was mutual.' Felipe leaned his head sideways to look into her downcast face. 'Come, it is not a tragedy.'

'It could be for Daddy. Don't you see? If Daddy is making himself ill worrying about Dale the shock of her running away might be fatal.'

Julie lowered her eyes from his as one tear fell into her lap followed by another. She was not even aware that they had come from her.

He said gently, 'You could be wrong. You were wrong about Dale and José. I take it that the delightful person in blue you greeted outside the hotel this afternoon was your mother?' Julie did not answer and he went on, 'I would like to meet her sometime in different circumstances.'

Julie knew that he was referring to Frank Braddon and she blinked away the tears as he knew she would on a change of subject. But she did not want him to be kind to her. Furthermore, she did not want him to meet her mother. Soon they would both be leaving the island for ever, for Julie could not see either of them wishing to return.

'How is Roddy?' she asked, taking a cue from him and changing the subject.

'Much better. He is coming out of hospital to-morrow.'

'I'm glad,' she answered. 'And now, if you'll excuse me, I'm dining with Mummy this evening.'

He rose to his feet to put out a hand to help her up. But she stood up unaided and walked normally despite her ankle back along the terrace.

'Would you rather I told your father about Dale?' he asked, suiting his long strides to her shorter ones.

'No, thank you.' Julie had never been nearer to bursting into tears. She went on with an effort, 'I'm very grateful to you for tracking down Dale so quickly. It means I can tell Daddy and so save a certain amount of gossip. Goodbye, Felipe.'

He took the hand she offered, and his smile was tender. 'Your father is a very lucky man to have a daughter who cares as much as you do. Some day I hope to be blessed with children like you. *Adios*, Julie.'

CHAPTER NINE

THROUGH a mist of tears, Julie watched Felipe slide into his car and drive away, and she was making her way into the hotel when she noticed the big car parked not far from where Felipe's had been. Frank Braddon was sitting in the driver's seat. He was too busy lighting a cigarette to notice her. His presence at the hotel could only mean that her mother had already gone inside to collect her to dine with them as arranged.

Her eyes scanned the foyer with people milling around, then she caught Tomas's eye at the reception desk. He beckoned. A lady had gone upstairs to her room but ten minutes ago, he told her.

Julie's first call was at her father's office. It was empty. So was the adjoining bedroom. She was leaving the office when voices reached her from the corridor outside. She did something then that she could never account for—diving back into the bedroom adjoining and pushing the door to leave a crack through which to peep.

The next moment her parents had entered the office.

Her mother was saying, 'Thanks for showing me around. I can't think where Julie has got to. You did say that she telephoned you earlier on to say that she was dining with me?'

'Yes. She's probably in the gardens. Sit down for a moment. She'll be back. Tomas will send her up.'

Through the crack in the door Julie saw her father draw out the chair facing his desk, knowing that she could hardly reveal her presence at this stage without some embarrassment.

Her mother sat on the edge of the chair rather nervously.

'I've left Frank waiting in the car. He'll wonder what's taking me so long,' she said.

'Can I offer you a drink while you're waiting?'

Her father was at the drinks cabinet fingering glasses and bottles. When the offer was declined he poured one out for himself, then leaned back against the cabinet to look down at his visitor.

Bluntly, he asked, 'Are you going to marry him?'

'Marry whom?'

'This friend of yours who brought you to the island?'

'I don't know. Surely you're not that interested?'

Her mother's voice, shaky at first, was gaining a cool steadiness. Her father took in a rasping breath.

'Of course I'm interested! Damn it, you were my wife. Will you tell me something honestly?' he said grimly.

'I wasn't aware that either of us lied to each other.'

'True,' he agreed. 'But a little straight talking wouldn't come amiss. Are you happy as you are?'

The answer came pat. 'I might ask the same of you. If being a success in life means anything then we should both be happy career-wise.'

'True again,' he replied even more grimly. 'But you still haven't answered my question. Are you happy?'

Her mother said wearily, 'What is happiness, a state of mind, a deep thankfulness for regular meals and a roof over one's head? I find life bearable because of Julie. How about you?'

He downed his drink in one gulp, set down the glass and thrust his hands into his pockets.

Forcibly, he said, 'Why exactly did you divorce me, Elizabeth? There was no other man.'

'Because you wanted me to.'

'I didn't—we just drifted too far apart.'

Her mother's voice was choked. 'And whose fault was that? Not mine. You were married to your job. I never saw you for weeks on end. Was it any wonder we became like strangers?'

'If you'd loved me you would have been overjoyed each time I returned home.'

'Overjoyed to be a kind of mistress—because that was what I was. You never consulted me in anything. I was there for your convenience.' Her mother laughed at her own stupidity. 'Do you know, I was dreadfully afraid of losing you because in the early days our marriage was wonderful. Then I gradually reached the stage of not caring any longer.'

His laugh was without mirth. 'Since we parted I've had lots of post-mortems on where I went wrong. You've put a new construction on it. Was I so selfish? Looking back, I suppose I was.'

A chair scraped back and Julie saw her mother rise to her feet. Her face was working as she cried passionately, 'What's the good of raking up the past? It's gone. The trouble is there'll never be anyone like you to me. It's ... been that way with me always, but you chose someone else.'

'No, you're wrong. Look, we have to talk.'

In the electric silence which followed Julie held her breath. Every pang, all the anguish brought on by the divorce was forgotten in the ecstatic hope that they would come together again. A joy so terrible that it squeezed her heart to a point of breathlessness surged over her.

But her mother was shaking her head. 'It's too late, Rick. Too late.'

'Please, Elizabeth!'

'I'm going to Julie's room to see if she's back. Goodbye, Rick.'

Her mother was in such a hurry to leave that she fled, leaving the office door leading into the corridor ajar. Julie stood in a kind of mental blackout for several moments, unable to move. Flung from such emotional heights, she was in no condition to act rationally.

She saw her father move slowly with the steps of an old, old man to drop heavily into his office chair where he dropped his head on his arms on the desk. Then she crept out of the bedroom with the knowledge that the door, left ajar by her mother's sudden departure, would give the impression of her having just walked in.

She went up to her father and touched his arm. 'Daddy, are you all right?' she asked gently.

His head shot up then and she was shattered. He looked dreadful.

'Where the devil have you been?' he snapped angrily. 'Your mother is waiting for you.'

Julie sat on the arm of his chair and placed an arm around his shoulders.

'I've news for you about Dale,' she said.

'What about Dale? You haven't been quarrelling, have you?'

'I think she's gone away,' Julie said carefully as he collected himself. 'Does the name Gerald Euston mean anything to you?'

He frowned thoughtfully. 'Euston? Yes. He had a yacht in the bay. Used to bring his guests to the hotel some evenings. José trained one or two of his race-horses.' He raised a brow. 'You mean he and Dale ...?'

She nodded. 'José told Felipe. Poor Daddy! Is it a big shock?'

She put her cheek against his head and hugged him.

'Well, I'm damned!' he exclaimed, and started to laugh.

'You mean you don't care?'

'Why should I? Dale has got what she wanted—a wealthy man.'

This was all too much for Julie. She was staring at him in blank surprise when her mother came in.

'Julie,' she cried, 'really! I've been searching everywhere for you. It's too bad of you to behave like this when you knew we were coming. I don't know what Frank is going to say keeping him waiting like this.'

Julie slipped from the arm of her father's chair. 'Sorry, Mummy—I'm ready when you are! I'll see you later, Daddy,' she whispered before following her mother from the office. 'I won't say anything about you know what until I see you again.'

Julie did not enjoy the evening out with her mother and Frank Braddon. The Hotel Splendide was new and luxurious, but it lacked the quaint elegance of the Jacarandas, with its marble-floored foyer and high-ceilinged rooms.

They had champagne and Frank brandished an expensive cigar when they retired for coffee on the terrace overlooking the sea. Julie did her best to keep up the conversation, but her heart was not in it. It was with her father, wondering how he really felt about Dale. One thing was certain: he had not known of Dale's departure when he had pleaded with her mother for them to talk. That being so, he was not trying to get her mother back because Dale had walked out on him.

She kept her promise not to say anything about Dale and parted on a low note with her mother.

Before she left Julie went with her mother to her hotel room to collect a present she had brought her from Madrid. The beautiful Spanish shawl, hand-painted, with a fabulous fringe, took Julie's breath away.

'It's gorgeous!' she gasped. 'Absolutely out of this

world! Thanks, Mummy.'

Flinging her arms around her mother's neck, she kissed her soft cheek.

'Wear it the next time you go out with your handsome Spaniard.'

Julie turned quickly away from her mother's tender smile to fold up the shawl and return it to the wrapping.

'I shan't be seeing Felipe again, Mummy. It won't be long now before we go home. Do you plan to stay on here?'

'Well, it is tempting, and a break away from work for me. In Madrid I was always conscious of being on a job. Here I'm not. I can relax. What about you?'

Julie said craftily, 'I shall love having you here with Daddy as well. It will be almost like old times. We did have good times together in the old days, didn't we, Mummy?'

The shawl now neatly wrapped, Julie took a quick glance at her mother's face to see it all closed up. 'I don't want to talk about it, Julie,' she said.

'But would you go back to Daddy if he asked you?' she persisted.

Julie's heart dropped at the sudden hardening of her mother's expression.

'Look, Julie, let's get this straight, shall we? Your father and I are divorced. Right? So let's have no more nonsense of a reconciliation. I want to enjoy myself while I'm here and I'm sure you do too. Let's do that, shall we?'

Upon returning to the Hotel Jacarandas, Julie sought out her father, to find him in his private suite. He had a dressing gown on and was listening to a record.

'Hello,' he said, reaching to turn off the sound. 'Have a good time?'

'So-so,' she replied, and sat down on to a comfortable chair to smile across the space between them. 'How are you feeling?'

'Fine,' he answered. 'I was just going to ring for a nightcap, a hot drink before bed. Like one?'

'Yes, please,' she answered, relieved to find him looking normal.

He reached for the telephone and ordered two hot drinks.

'I've been doing some enquiring while you were out. I telephoned Felipe and José, who both confirmed your story about Dale. Some of her clothes are gone, but she didn't leave a note. I wonder why?'

'Perhaps she thought you might have prevented her from going if she had.'

He shook his head. 'I don't think so.'

'How extraordinary,' Julie commented. 'I don't get it.'

'You would if you knew all the details, but I'm too weary to talk about them tonight. Going out with your mother tomorrow?'

'Yes. We're going to do some sightseeing.' She was hugging her present and saw him glance at it. 'Mummy bought me a Spanish shawl. Like to see it?'

He shook his head. 'Some other time. I'm sure it must be very pretty. Your mother always had excellent taste.'

He called out in answer to a tap on the door and one of the staff entered with their drinks. They sat for some time sipping them in silence, then her father said,

'Felipe doesn't think much of this man your mother is friends with. What do you think about him?'

Julie shrugged slim shoulders. 'I'm not wildly enthusiastic, but it's none of our business, is it, whom Mummy chooses for her friends. Frank has been kind to her and I suppose she appreciates it.'

'Felipe has been kind to you, but you aren't reciprocating in the same way.'

That's all you know, Julie thought despairingly. Aloud she said, 'Felipe is Spanish, with an entirely different outlook.'

Her father stared down into his drink. 'His sentiments are similar, but Felipe is a man of integrity. I believe he's contemplating matrimony in any case.'

Julie's heart plunged into the depths. 'Really? With whom? Sharon?'

He smiled wryly. 'No. Apparently she's a distant relation of his, a very pretty girl of about nineteen. He met her at the airport this evening accompanied by her mother. He called here with them to show them the changes. They remembered the Jacarandas when it was a villa.'

Julie's voice was little more than a croak. 'I suppose she's well educated and wealthy?' she quipped on a mound of pain.

'I would think so. She lives in Madrid.'

Julie thought idiotically, if I'd gone to join Mummy in Madrid I might have met her. Better that I didn't. I don't want to see the girl Felipe has chosen for his wife. She had the feeling of being shot to pieces.

'I'm going to bed,' she said with an effort. 'I'm tired and I'm sure you are. See you in the morning.'

She stood up on trembling legs, put down her cup and kissed the top of his head. She did not remember going to her room. She found herself in the centre of her bedroom trying to sort out a jumbled pattern of thoughts. The sensible thing to do was to face life as it came. What if Felipe did marry his Spanish sweetheart? What if her mother did marry Frank? Life had to go on.

There was her father—he would need her now Dale had gone. With a long sigh and shivering a little with apprehension, Julie dragged herself across the room and back to the present. She was a long time going to sleep, an uneasy sleep broken in the end by the ringing of the telephone by the bed.

Forcing open one sleepy eyelid to look at the small illuminated travel clock beside the bed, she groped for the telephone receiver. It was Roddy.

'Do you know what time it is?' she snapped. 'Two-thirty in the morning!'

'Sorry.' Roddy sounded anything but. 'I rang earlier, but you were out. What about coming over tomorrow? I'm O.K. Felipe has lent me one of his cars, so I can pick you up if you like.'

Julie told him that she was going out with her mother but was happy to know that he was better. He reminded her that she owed him a day in lieu of the one following the accident. A day in her company was, in his opinion, too precious to lose.

'I'll let you know when I can make it,' she promised. 'Meanwhile, what about dating some Spanish *señorita?*'

He sounded very hurt. 'You don't mean it?' he protested.

'Why not?' she reasoned. 'You're on holiday.'

He rang off abruptly and Julie snuggled down into bed. The easiest way to forget one's problems was to take on someone else's, she thought sleepily. She was all for helping Roddy to mature gently, but it was difficult to know exactly what to do.

She had breakfast brought to her room next morning, she was late rising and had to dash. Lucia brought golden brown curly cakes of crisp bread dusted with sugar and delicious with butter and honey spread on liberally. Lucia poured out the coffee while Julie drank her fruit juice.

She caught the bus into Palma by the skin of her

teeth and saw her mother waiting for her at the terminal. That first morning they were content to stroll around the shops and take a leisurely mid-morning drink at one of the many outside cafés along the tree-shaded Borne.

Julie refused to allow visions of Felipe with his Spanish bride-to-be spoil her day, so it came as something of a shock to come across him in the restaurant they went to for lunch.

'Splashing out a bit, aren't we, Mummy?' she whispered as they went into the sparkling, expensive dining room. 'We'd better go Dutch.'

'No, we won't,' her mother assured her. 'It isn't as expensive as it looks. Frank recommended it.'

Julie went off the place immediately. 'You mean it's one of his places?'

'No. It's run by a Spanish family and many of the locals come here.'

The place was filling up rapidly as they were shown to their table by a smart waiter who beamed upon them with approval.

Glancing around the room, Julie noticed two women coming in. The girl was very striking with dark eyes set in an oval face. The features were not perfect, the narrow nose was too long, the mouth a little too full, but the smooth black hair with the sheen of a raven's wing gave her face a singular beauty. There was no doubt that the woman accompanying her was her mother, for there was a distinct similarity of features.

'How extraordinary!' Julie's mother was staring at the two women in surprise. 'That girl and her mother who've just come in are friends of mine. I met them in Madrid, at a fashion show. And look, they're with your Spanish heart-throb—Felipe, did you say his name was?'

Julie stared in dismay at the tall figure in a cream safari suit, dark brown silk shirt and cream tie who was walking behind them with elegant ease. He smiled charmingly at the head waiter who hurried forward to greet them and the party came towards Julie and her mother.

Desperately Julie whispered, 'Goodness, they're coming this way! Can't we duck under the table or something?'

Her mother chuckled. 'Whatever for? I've been wanting to meet a really dishy Spaniard, and your Felipe is about as dishy as they can get.'

'He's not my Felipe,' Julie retorted crossly.

Somehow her lips were smiling when Felipe stopped to greet them.

'This is indeed a surprise, Julie,' said Felipe, glancing at her mother, who was eyeing him with interest.

'Yes, isn't it?' Julie replied. 'Mummy, this is Felipe de Torres y Aquiliño, a friend of Daddy. Felipe, my mother, Elizabeth Denver.'

He greeted her mother charmingly. 'Delighted to meet you. Welcome to the island.'

'Thank you,' Mrs Denver cooed, and her smile included the two Spanish women. 'Lovely to see you again so soon.'

Felipe's black eyebrows shot up in surprise. 'You ladies have met before?'

'Indeed we have. Señora de Lesconda, Señorita Margalida, this is my daughter Julie.'

'Dear Elizabeth,' Señora de Lesconda murmured. 'I am much too matronly in figure to be mistaken for anyone other than a *madre*. But you could easily be mistaken to be a sister to your daughter. What a pretty child she is! Do you not agree, Felipe?'

The dark eyes flicked impersonally over Julie's blushing face.

'But certainly, *señora*,' he replied smoothly, and gave his attention to the hovering waiter, eager to show them to their table.

'We shall see you again.' Felipe was smiling. 'Perhaps you will come to dine with us one evening?'

'We would be delighted,' Julie's mother replied.

As Felipe and his party moved on Julie gave a sigh of relief. Nevertheless she was shattered. It had happened. She had met Felipe's future bride. Her mother was saying,

'Señora de Lesconda and her daughter were very kind to me and I was invited to their villa on the outskirts of Madrid several times. Señor de Lesconda is a charming man. It was he who told me that his daughter Margalida was engaged to someone in Majorca.'

Julie listened and at the same time tried to be fatalistic about Felipe. She had not wanted to see him again, finding his absence preferable to the torture of his presence. Now she was to have the shattering experience of seeing the man she loved being utterly charming and attentive to the girl of his heart.

From her table she had a good view of Margalida's face glowing with a soft peach-like bloom, her full lips red as cherries. Julie tortured herself wondering how often Felipe had kissed them, and the length of the Spanish meal stretched almost beyond endurance. When it was over Julie jostled her mother out before Felipe and his party had finished eating.

They spent the afternoon on a pleasure cruise, after which Julie tried to persuade her mother to go back with her to the Hotel Jacarandas for the evening.

'Sorry, dear,' she said, 'but I promised to have dinner with Frank this evening. Why not stay and eat with us?'

'No, thanks.'

Julie tormented herself with a picture of her mother and Frank Braddon dining intimately by candlelight on her return to the hotel. As if she had not enough to contend with!

She washed and changed and went along to see her father in his private suite. His greeting was so bright that she was partially soothed. He told her without emotion that he had received a telephone call from Dale telling him that she had gone away with Gerald Euston, and in the next breath he asked Julie how she had enjoyed her day out with her mother.

They dined downstairs in the restaurant and Julie wondered with concern whether or not her father was now going to plunge himself into his job once again in order to forget Dale. Mentally she was wringing her hands over the whole tragic situation.

Conversation did not come easily to either of them. When Julie was not looking at her father's sober countenance, she was seeing her mother dining with Frank Braddon. They were at the coffee stage when she told him about seeing Felipe with his Margalida.

He said teasingly, 'Didn't seeing Felipe with his *novia* make you want one of your own?'

Unknowingly he was pushing the knife in further and twisting it until Julie writhed in pain.

She said passionately, 'Why should I saddle myself with a man, only to end up like you and Mummy?'

He looked at her with concern. 'Steady on, my dear! In our case it was just one of those things,' he said helplessly.

'You bet it was!'

She could not go on; her throat was blocked with tears. Hardly aware of what she was doing, she pushed back her chair and fled. A strange coldness spread over her from head to toe as she leaned back against the closed door of her room. Blinking away the tears, she decided to pack her case and go. But to where? To her mother and Frank Braddon ... the man who might take her father's place, who even now could be kissing her mother.

Suddenly reckless, tearing anger gave her strength. She was going to make one last desperate attempt to bring her parents together, and she was going to ask Felipe to help. Why not? He owed her something for ensnaring her with his charms.

She telephoned his farm and waited with bated breath for his voice.

'Hello, Felipe, this is Julie. Will you do me a favour? Will you invite Mummy and Daddy to your place one evening but don't let either of them know that the other is coming?'

Felipe sounded amused. 'Will you be coming also?'

'Yes, please.'

She went on to tell him of her plan to get her parents together in the hope that they would sort things out. Felipe agreed wholeheartedly.

'I happen to be giving a small dinner party tomorrow evening. Will that suit you?'

'That will be fine. I'm sure Mummy will come and I can let Daddy think that just he and I have been invited. I shan't mention Mummy.'

'Then I will contact your mother immediately.'

Already Julie was beginning to feel more calm. 'Thank you, Felipe,' she said, adding thoughtfully, 'It won't interfere with any plans you've made, will it?'

A pause. 'On the contrary, it will fit in with them nicely,' he replied laconically.

Julie put down the telephone wondering what kind of fish he was intent upon frying. Whatever it was it could not have anything to do with her. If he was planning to announce his engagement then she would have to bear it. Meanwhile she would live in the hope that she would have the support of united parents.

The telephone rang as she was moving away from it.

'Are you all right, dear?' her father asked anxiously. 'You and I must have a talk sometime.'

'I'm sorry, Daddy. You have enough troubles of your own—which reminds me, who will help out on reception now Dale has gone?'

'No one as yet. Why?'

'Then let me help until you find someone.'

'But you're on holiday.'

'So what? I could do a few hours tomorrow morning. I can go out later with Mummy. Please, Daddy!'

CHAPTER TEN

JULIE was almost happy to have persuaded her father to let her help out at reception as a relief for Tomas until someone suitable was found to take Dale's place. She would not feel normal until the day was over and her parents met at Felipe's party that evening.

Felipe must have telephoned her mother immediately after she had asked him. She had been preparing for bed when her mother had rung her up. She said Felipe had not only invited them to a party at his house the following evening, he was sending a car for her. It would make a difference to their plans since she would be having her hair done some time the next day.

Julie suggested them meeting at the party since she was helping out on reception for a few hours as something had come up and her father was shorthanded. She did not tell her mother about Dale going. If everything went well that evening her father would do all the explaining.

Her father was again taking up his duties around the hotel and Felipe called mid-morning accompanied by an elderly man whom he introduced as a possible assistant in the running of the hotel. Julie thought her father looked brighter at lunch time. He was quite enthusiastic over the new arrival.

'Trust Felipe to step in diplomatically and help,' he said. 'An assisant manager will be a boon. Incidentally, Felipe has invited us to a party he's giving this evening.'

Julie managed to put on a look of surprise. 'That's lovely,' she said. 'We are going, aren't we, Daddy?'

'I can hardly refuse, can I, now I have someone to leave in charge. Besides, I haven't taken you about as I should have done.'

Julie prepared for the party that evening in a state of excitement. Until now the thought of the consequences of involving herself emotionally had not occurred. She had been too obsessed with thinking about the possible reunion of her parents.

It was only when she was actually on her way to the party with her father in his car that she began to realise what she might have let herself in for. She could find herself having to congratulate Felipe on his engagement to Margalida. She went cold at the thought, then pulled herself together impatiently. A last effort had to be made to bring her parents together, regardless of the consquences to herself.

Her father was saying pensively, 'I would like to see you engaged to some nice chap instead of roaming around footloose and fancy free. I shall worry about you until you're settled.'

Julie stole a glance at his profile. 'What about you? You're practically free now, so I shall be worrying about you as well as Mummy.'

He said evenly, 'Why should you worry about your mother?'

'Because I'd hate her to marry Frank Braddon. He isn't her kind of man.'

There was a long pause, then he said, 'Is she going out with him this evening?'

'I hope not,' said Julie fervently.

Her father did not reply, and soon they were arriving at Felipe's delightful home where he greeted them cordially, looking dangerously attractive in evening dress. His smile at Julie was mocking as he greeted her. Almost at once Roddy was there, looking remarkably fit after his accident, and as he drew her away to a secluded corner she saw Margalida, and her mother in brown and wine silk respectively, across the *salón*.

The *salón* was rapidly filling with guests as they collided with Grace and Stanley Main who thanked Julie for her timely visit to Roddy at the time of his accident. Then with Roddy sticking by her side, Julie moved on.

José was there with his aunt Doña Conchita, whose chair was surrounded by friends. Julie quivered on the thought that this was no ordinary party since Doña Conchita was making one of her rare appearances in public, and she looked round apprehensively for her mother.

Roddy was excitedly extolling the virtues of the car which Felipe had lent him and was outlining plans for a day out when Julie saw her mother walk into the *salón* with Felipe. The next moment her father had joined them and with Felipe between them they all left the room.

Excusing herself to Roddy, Julie went in search of the powder room, feeling the need to be on her own in what she considered were the most crucial moments of her life. Whatever her parents' decision was she had to accept it. So it was with this in mind that she returned to mingle among the guests and look for Felipe.

Presently she saw him at the far side of the room and hurried across. The hand she laid on his arm was trembling and all she could do was to look up at him imploringly.

'I have left your parents together in the small *sala*,' he told her. 'I will take you there in due course.'

Julie recoiled in horror at the thought. 'No, Felipe,' she protested. 'Whatever happens they must never know that I had a hand in trying to bring them together.' Her look at him was piteous. 'Do you think there's any hope?'

'There is always hope.' He looked at her, smiling a little though he spoke seriously. 'One never gives up hope under any conditions.'

For a second his hand rested on hers as it rested tremblingly on his arm, then Roddy was there and Felipe moved away to mingle with his other guests.

Roddy said, 'I've been in the dining room to make sure I've been put next to you at dinner, and I'm not letting you go tonight until we've made a date for our next meeting.'

Julie regarded him with some dismay, hoping that he was not taking their relationship too seriously. Then she realised that she must not become serious herself.

Playfully, she said, 'That was rash of you, Roddy. Who knows, you might have been sitting by a beautiful Spanish *señorita*?'

He looked at her seriously, his young face set. 'We are playing games, aren't we, Julie? Look, what exactly is going on?'

'I don't know what you mean, Roddy,' she replied. 'What could be going on at a perfectly enchanting party?'

'Exactly,' he said grimly. 'First I see your parents who are divorced leaving the room with Felipe and him coming back alone. And where's Dale?'

He had taken her arm and pulled her along with him to a corner of the room behind a banked-up flower display near to the door.

'I can't tell you anything yet, Roddy,' she said piteously. 'I don't know myself.'

Fiercely he demanded, 'Is that why you went to Felipe just now looking as if your world had suddenly come to an end?'

'Perhaps it has,' she said with a vain attempt at lightness.

But it did not work with Roddy. 'Then there is something going on. I knew when I first met you that you weren't happy, that there was some load you were carrying around with you.' His eyes narrowed down at her pale face. 'You came to Majorca with the idea of bringing your parents together again, didn't you?'

'No, I did not,' she told him firmly and frankly. 'And let go of my arm, you're hurting.'

Roddy released her immediately, contrite and pleading. He said, 'Let's go for a run in the car and eat somewhere cosy and quiet. I've no interest in this party and I know you haven't. Please, Julie?'

She regarded him with hostile eyes as she massaged the arm he had gripped.

'How do you know I haven't?' she said grimly.

He shrugged youthful wide shoulders. 'Damn it, how can you? I for one don't want to sit listening to the announcement of someone else's engagement when I'm practically grovelling at a certain person's dainty feet.'

Julie went paler. 'But you can't mean ... that you ...?'

He nodded soberly. 'That's right. You know I'm crazy about you?'

Julie shook her head dumbly. 'You're being unfair, Roddy. I never gave you that much encouragement. Just because we get on well together it doesn't mean we were made for each other.'

He teetered on the edge of anger. 'You talk of being unfair?' he accused. 'What about poor Dale, plotting things behind her back?'

'You don't know what you're talking about,' she cried. 'Bother Dale!'

He brought his set face nearer to hers. 'I suppose it's bother Roddy as well, is it?'

'You know it isn't.' Julie's heart was thundering as she gazed at his working face. 'I like you very much,

Roddy, but only as a friend. You're far too young to form any lasting attachment yet.'

She twisted the silken cord of the evening purse on her arm as she tried to let him down lightly.

'O.K. We're going to be the best of friends while we learn more about each other,' he said. 'Come on, let's go. I'll wait for you outside while you fetch your wrap.'

Julie hung back. 'What about Sharon? She'll expect you to stay.'

He frowned. 'What has she to do with it? She isn't getting engaged.'

She looked at him in dismay. Poor Sharon, she thought, I know what she must be going through at this moment. It was on the tip of her tongue to tell him that it was Sharon whom he ought to be taking out in the car to save the poor girl the ordeal of seeing the man she loved announcing his engagement to someone else.

Margalida. Felipe. Of course! Julie panicked. Seeing them engaged and possibly seeing the plan to bring her parents together fall through was more than she was prepared to face all at once. There could be no harm in going out with Roddy and then returning to wait while he found out for her about her parents.

Seated beside Roddy, Julie could not forget that the car they were in belonged to Felipe, that he also had occupied the driving seat. But she refused to dwell upon Felipe or her parents until she had to. This outing with Roddy could well be her last since she was not staying long on the island anyway.

Roddy drove fast along quiet roads through the stretching groves of lemons and vines, then swung off the main road to a restaurant overlooking the bay. The meal they had was excellent, but Julie did not taste a thing. Her thoughts kept going back to the farm where

Felipe would be preparing himself for the announcement of his engagement to Margalida.

She said, 'I hope our absence from the farm won't be noticed too much.'

Roddy shrugged it off. 'Couples are doing it all the time at parties.'

'But Felipe is a friend, and you're one of his guests,' she insisted.

He said carelessly, 'Felipe will be too busy looking after the engaged couple to bother about us.'

Julie found a difficulty in breathing. 'What ... what did you say?' she croaked. 'Who is getting engaged, exactly?'

Roddy refilled her wine glass then his own. 'Didn't you know?' he asked with an aggravating slowness. 'Why, José and Margalida. It seems that they've been engaged for years, an arrangement between their families in true Spanish fashion.'

He raised a brow as he saw the colour rush to her face.

'Don't tell me you didn't know?' he said.

Julie looked and felt bemused. 'But I thought Felipe ...'

She broke off to look at him helplessly and he grinned.

'You mean Felipe and Margalida? Not a hope. Now if you'd said Felipe and Sharon.'

'You mean they ...?'

Julie could not go on. She watched Roddy tucking into his succulent steak and pushed her own away, having lost her appetite for it.

He chewed, had another drink of wine and went on. 'Your guess is as good as mine. Sharon likes Felipe, I know that. Our parents like him too.'

So it was Sharon, Julie thought. Then Roddy was speaking again.

'About tomorrow—what time can I pick you up?'

Julie looked at him without taking in what he had said, and he waved a hand in front of her eyes across the table.

'I said what about us going out tomorrow,' he repeated. 'Are you in a brown study?'

She gave a start, said wearily, 'Oh, Roddy, I can't—I don't know what Mummy has planned for us.'

'I shall call for you all the same. I'd rather have your mother tagging along than not have your company,' he threatened.

But Julie was in another brown study, this time about José.

The reason for Doña Conchita being at the party was clear. It had been her dearest wish for José to marry and settle down. Now he had agreed to marry his childhood *novia* his aunt would, no doubt, lend him the money to extend his stables elsewhere on the island.

Looking back, that evening had a special dreamlike quality about it to Julie. The breathtaking view over the sea, the trees, the winding roads, the sleeping narrow winding little streets in the villages, the silent shuttered villas with their beautiful gardens spilling over with flowers drifted by like framed pictures through the window of the car when they returned to Felipe's farmhouse.

The courtyard and galleried house as the car swept in enhanced the feeling of unreality, of entering another world, but a more romantic one nevertheless.

At Julie's urgent request, Roddy went indoors to see what he could learn about her parents and if they were still there. She had not long to wait before he was back, to slip in the car beside her.

'According to Sharon,' he said, 'your parents left not

long ago together. So you'll probably want to go home
to the hotel.'

'Yes, please, Roddy,' she answered.

They were on their way when Roddy spoke again.
He appeared to be subdued, his voice lacklustre.

'I have further news for you,' he told her. 'Apparently the party this evening served a double purpose,
the engagement and a farewell gesture to my family and
myself. We're leaving tomorrow afternoon to continue
on our world cruise. However, it will only be a tem-
porary parting for us and Felipe. He's hinted that it's
more than likely that he'll see us later in the States.'

Julie stared down at the little evening purse on her
arm unseeingly.

'Did you see Felipe?' she asked in a low voice.

'No. He was with Doña Conchita, José, Margalida
and her mother. Sharon said that Felipe had told my
parents that he was going to be extremely busy for the
next month or so, but that we should all meet again in
the future in the States.'

'I'm sorry you're going, Roddy, but I shall be going
myself soon. Are your family very disappointed at being
asked to go?'

'Not really. They only stopped over their time because of Sharon. I'm the one who's shattered because
I'm leaving you. I don't suppose we could meet tomorrow morning for a last drink together?'

Julie shook her head. 'I don't think so. It's been nice
knowing you and we might meet again some day. I've
had a wonderful evening,' she said sincerely.

But how much more wonderful, her heart cried, had
Felipe been there instead of Roddy. Then because it
made her feel ungrateful she looked penitently at him
as he pulled up outside the hotel.

Putting up her hand, she caressed his cheek and
leaned over to kiss him. It seemed to her in one brief

moment that he was too shy to respond. Then he was
kissing her in the way she had meant him to, kissing
her until she was breathless.

Julie was the first to pull away. 'Dear Roddy,' she
said on breath regained. 'Kiss the girl you fall in love
with like that and you'll win her! You're going to be
quite a guy. Goodbye.'

Before he could move she had left the car and had
gone into the hotel, leaving him staring after her.

She made her way slowly into the hotel with her
fingers crossed. Had her parents made it up or would
she find her father looking the way he had of late, des-
pondent and unhappy? She made her way first to his
office and was relieved to discover that he was not
there.

They were waiting for her in the private suite, looking so happy that a lump rose in her throat. No need
to ask if they were together again. It showed in their
faces and the tender smiles they greeted her with.

Julie ran to her mother to throw her arms around
her neck.

'Oh, Mummy,' she cried, 'you are going to be together again, aren't you, you and Daddy?'

'Yes, dear, we are,' her mother replied, kissing her
wet cheek.

Her father was at the drinks cabinet pouring them
all a drink by way of celebration. He looked years
younger and there was a spring in his step as he came
forward with the drinks on a tray.

'To us,' he said, as they raised their glasses.

'Daddy, champagne?' Julie cried, her eyes sparkling
no less than the bubbly liquid in her glass.

'Why not?' he replied.

She sighed and sat on the arm of her mother's chair
as her father beamed down upon them. In her moment
of supreme happiness, she spared a thought for Dale

... who had taken her father away and had now given him back.

Generously, she lifted the remainder of champagne in her glass and said, 'To Dale. Let's hope she eventually finds happiness.'

'To Dale.'

Julie turned to her mother when the toast had been drunk.

'Dale wasn't a bad sort of girl. I like her in spite of everything. She had her good points, like us all.'

'I agree,' her mother said wholeheartedly. 'Now, your father has something to show you.'

For several seconds Julie stared at the cablegram her father gave her. It was to the effect that Dale had been married that morning.

Her look of bewilderment included them both. 'But I don't understand,' she protested. 'How can Dale marry again before a divorce has been gone through?'

'Perfectly simple,' her father explained. 'We were never married. There was never anything between us. When Dale knew I was coming here she begged me to take her with me. She wanted to get away in order to have a chance of what she called a good marriage. When we came here we realised that it would be much simpler if we pretended to be married in order to give the job the respectability it needed.'

He moved slowly to the window. 'I went along with the deception with the prime motive of protecting Dale from impulsive decisions which might have proved detrimental to her future happiness. We were never lovers. I knew I had to get away and I counted upon support from my own family which I didn't get.' He gave a short bitter laugh. 'We British are supposed to be a liberated race, yet we aren't. We're still narrow-minded enough to misjudge.'

He turned round slowly. 'And where did you disappear to, Julie, earlier this evening? It wasn't a very nice thing to do to Felipe as your host.'

Julie said frankly, 'I had to get away. I dreaded the thought that you two wouldn't become reconciled. Besides, Roddy and I have been such good friends, and they're leaving tomorrow.' Suddenly she brightened. 'I've just realised something. You two can marry again at any time. Isn't that wonderful?'

Her father said darkly, teasingly, 'It still doesn't get you off the hook, young lady. I've never seen Felipe so angry. I'm sure he would have cheerfully wrung your pretty little neck for behaving so rudely as to leave his party without so much as an excuse-me.'

'I know, and I'm sorry,' she admitted. 'I'll write him a little note.'

Dryly her father said, 'I think the situation calls for more than some words scrawled on paper. You owe it to him to apologise personally.'

Julie looked shattered. 'But I couldn't, Daddy. I just couldn't!'

'Why not, darling?' her mother queried gently. 'You'll get it over much quicker than sitting pondering over a polite little note.'

'Very well, I'll do that,' Julie agreed, knowing that she would find some way of getting out of it. She added brightly,

'Have you decided what you're going to do?'

Her mother nodded. 'Yes, we have, dear. We're going home to be remarried as soon as possible. Everybody here believes that your father is legally married to Dale.'

'And after that?' Julie asked.

Her father answered. 'We haven't thought that far as yet. We shall be leaving as soon as possible. The news of Dale's mariage is sure to hit the headlines in the press because her husband is a wealthy industrialist and people would only talk if they saw your mother and me together.'

'I'd like to come with you,' Julie said eagerly.

But her father did not agree. 'There's not the slightest reason why you shouldn't finish your holiday, my dear. The new under-manager will carry on very satisfactorily in my place.'

Julie said reasonably, 'I couldn't stay when Dale's marriage is made known.'

'Julie is right, Rick,' put in her mother. 'Better make that plane reservation for three.'

Later Julie lay in bed with sleep very far away. It had been quite a memorable evening where she was concerned, a time of celebration and a time for sorrow. But she would not be greedy. In addition to having her parents back she had known what it was like to be really in love. Something soul-shattering had happened to her which would remain with her for the rest of her life. Part of her would always belong to Felipe, making it impossible to offer herself to any other man as a whole person.

Her father would be staying up half the night putting the assistant manager right about his job, as they were leaving the following afternoon for home.

Her mother had gone back to her hotel and they were to pick her up on the way to the airport. Julie could not wait to be gone, gone away from Felipe, from those clear-cut disturbingly handsome features, those dark eyes veiling feelings in which she knew she had no part, from that well-cut mouth with its mobility of heart-warming charm.

She went to sleep eventually with his image in her thoughts.

CHAPTER ELEVEN

THEY were ready to go. Everything had been packed, Julie's case was in the trunk of her father's car along with his and the note she had written to Felipe apologising for her behaviour at his party had been posted. He would not receive it until the following day. There had been no word from him and Julie guessed that he was as busy as he had told his American guests he would be. Doing what she had no idea, but she thought it was strange that he had made no move to say goodbye to them.

Her father had intimated that he might be saying goodbye to them at the airport along with Roddy and his family or she might never see him again having said his goodbyes to her parents the previous evening at his party.

Julie did not think she could bear saying goodbye to him and it was agony waiting until such time as they would go. The hotel staff had been told that her father was going on a holiday, so his departure was not an emotional one where they were concerned. After lunch Julie took a last stroll along the terrace, the scene of most of her encounters with Felipe. She lingered for some time, longing that her yearning for him would bring him in person. At last, with an irrational sense of disappointment she roused herself to retrace her steps with a heavy heart.

Tomas intercepted her on the way to her room. He was carrying a bouquet of dark red roses which he gave her with a wide smile.

'For you, Miss Julie,' he said. 'A messenger brought

them. There is a card attached.'

It was tucked among the flowers and her fingers trembled as they detached it. It read, 'A pleasant journey, Julie. *Vaya con Dios.* Felipe.'

She stood for several moments staring at it and trying to control her emotions.

'Is everything all right, miss?'

She gave a start, realised that Tomas was still there and said, 'Yes, thanks, Tomas. What does *Vaya con Dios*, mean?'

'It means go with God, Miss Julie.'

'Thank you, Tomas.' Julie had to turn away quickly before he saw the sudden tears. Hurrying to her room, Julie did not stop until she was inside leaning back against the closed door.

'Felipe. Oh, Felipe!' her heart cried with a tormenting vision of his handsome dark face and flashing smile.

The love of her life was over with a prayer and a bouquet of red roses. The future stretched before her, not blossoming into something wonderful with Felipe but narrowing, dwindling, and shrinking into a barren existence without him.

'Ready, Julie?'

Her father's peremptory tap on her door roused her and she began to gather her things together mechanically.

'Roses?' her father queried as she slid into the car with them.

'From Felipe,' she answered with a forced brightness. 'I'll sit in the back seat and leave Mummy to sit beside you. I just love seeing you together. I can't believe it even now.'

She spoke a half truth, as she wanted to be alone. Later on the plane she hoped to have gained a sense of normality. There was no sign of Roddy or his family at the airport, and Julie found herself looking round for them despite her determination to shut everything from her mind.

They would not be there, otherwise Felipe would not have sent the flowers. Their luggage was being checked in when the voice on the loudspeaker came loud and clear.

'Will Miss Julie Denver please come at once to the enquiry desk. Miss Julie Denver. Thank you.'

She turned a look of bewilderment upon her parents, and her father grinned.

'Roddy, probably,' he said. 'You'd better go, my dear.'

The pretty girl at the enquiry desk escorted Julie to one of the small offices used by the staff, opened the door and closed it after her with a sweet smile.

The tall wide-shouldered figure turned from the window as she entered and the colour left her face. Her heart gave a sickening lurch.

'Felipe!' she cried. 'I... I never expected to see you ... not after sending the flowers. Th-thank you, they were lovely.'

She broke off from her babbling, wishing that she could have been prepared for such a meeting. However, it was only a farewell procedure and it had to be gone through, a farewell to her life and happiness.

'You expected to see Roddy? Is that why you look so shattered? He appears to have made a conquest,' he said dryly. 'Even so, was it necessary for you to leave my party last evening so you could be together?'

Julie bit hard on her lip, having forced a measure of composure. She had not advanced far into the room and stood nervously fingering the strap of her shoulder bag.

She said quietly, 'That wasn't the reason I went with Roddy, and I've sent you a letter with my apologies for leaving the party. I know it was rude of me, but I had to do it.'

'Why?' he demanded sharply. 'Did you wish to annoy me?'

'No, no, it wasn't like that at all.'

Julie felt her composure slipping as he came slowly towards her.

He said, 'You mean you did not think of me at all?'

She shook her head. 'I was thinking of my parents and how I was going to bear it if they didn't come together again. I ... I was a bit of a coward, so I went out with Roddy until they'd made their decision. I sent Roddy to find out what it was when we got back.'

'Why did you not come to see me when you returned instead of going back to the hotel?'

'Roddy said you were busy with Doña Conchita and José. He also told me that he and his family were leaving because you'd be very busy for some time with affairs that demanded your attention.'

He said stiffly, 'That is so.' He had now moved right up to her and he was looking at her through narrowed eyes. 'You look upset. If it is about Roddy I can tell you that he and his family left but an hour ago. He left a message. He is going to write to you.'

Julie was finding his nearness more than she could bear, and she could not control her trembling.

'Niña, you are pale and trembling. Do not take on so.'

His voice and his hands were gentle as he took her by the shoulders. 'If it will help I will take Roddy's place. I will kiss you goodbye. So.'

Julie was beyond words. Her heart stopped beating, turned over, then raced on like a mad thing. She was shaking her head, yet her head was not moving as he bent his. His lips were gentle at first, then his kisses deepened and his arms tightened. Her arms lifted to go up around his neck, and she gave herself up to the ecstasy of being held in beloved arms.

It was several minutes before he lifted his head and her arms fell from around his neck. Flung from such emotional heights, Julie fought hard to keep her composure. Her heart was beating like a sledgehammer and she was sure he could hear it.

'You're a nice man, Felipe,' she began. 'Thanks for trying to console me. You do it very well. But I wasn't upset because Roddy had gone.'

Then why were you upset, *pequeña*?' he whispered, still holding her in his arms.

The eyes she lifted to his were wide with anguish. 'Oh, Felipe,' she sighed, 'you must know by now. I can't put it into words. It would be so embarrassing for us both.'

'Try me,' he said. He was smiling, all fire and kinetic magnetism, as he drew her closer.

'I can't. After all, you're going to the States later on and you wouldn't go all that distance if ... if you weren't in love with her. Why else would you go if not to see Sharon?'

'Why else indeed? I had planned a brief stop there while on my honeymoon—yours and mine. I love you, *pequeña*. Now tell me that you love me.'

For the second time in five minutes Julie had difficulty in breathing.

'I can't believe it,' she said. 'You see, I love you so much, Felipe. You don't know how much. It was one of the reasons why I ran away from your party. I couldn't stay to hear you announce your engagement to Margalida.' She laughed, near to tears. 'Then I thought it was Sharon who had your love. I just can't believe you love me.'

'Not even when I kissed you just now?' he teased mockingly with a wicked smile.

'I didn't dare believe it. Please convince me some

more,' she pleaded drowningly.

Her arms stole around his neck as he swept her close. Ardent moments passed as she felt herself lifted up above all earthly things. It was like meeting the full heat of the sun, this agony of joy as he kissed her with a passion which no longer left her in any doubt about his love for her.

Her cheeks were a warm smooth rose when he released her sufficiently to look up into his adoring eyes.

'Darling,' she said huskily. 'One thing puzzles me about my parents. They seemed to have settled their differences so quickly, and I think you had a hand in it.'

'Quite simple really. I told them that I wanted their daughter's hand in marriage and that it would make things easier all round if they were married also for our wedding.'

'And they never said anything about it. The only thing Daddy said was that it was just possible that you would be seeing us off at the airport. Oh, goodness, I'll miss the plane!'

Felipe consulted his watch, then replaced his arm around her. 'We have plenty of time,' he assured her coolly. 'Everything has been taken care of, has been for some time. I won't say that Dale's unexpected elopement did not precipitate matters, but I have no argument about that since it has brought us together a little sooner.'

Julie revelled in the fact that she could look up at him with all her love there for him to see.

'But Roddy said you'll be very busy during the next few months.'

'A honeymoon should keep one busy. Do you not agree?'

He laughed at the deepening colour in her face as he spoke teasingly.

'Incidentally,' he went on, 'José is going to manage the farm for me. He has always envied me the farm, so he will be quite happy stepping into my shoes. We shall probably come over for his wedding. But first we shall see him at our wedding in Cadiz.' He raised a brow. 'You agree to it being soon?'

She laughed up at him and nodded, and he had to sweep her close to demonstrate that it could not be too soon for him.

The air stewardess who looked in on them beamed. 'Your plane, Señor Aquiliño, Miss Denver,' she said.

They were following her along the corridors to catch up with the other passengers making their way to the plane when Julie smiled up at Felipe as she held his hand.

She said, 'She thinks you're going with us, darling. I wish you were.'

'I am,' laconically.

'You are?' Julie laughed from sheer happiness. 'Nobody tells me anything! Oh, I love you!'

Felipe lifted the hand clasped in his and kissed it.

He said, 'Your parents are to be remarried in London, then we all go on to my ancestral home in Cadiz. I'm afraid our wedding will be a big affair. Shall you mind?'

'Mind?' she echoed swooningly while trying to take it all in—her parents reunited, Felipe declaring his love for her, their wedding in Cadiz. The wide eyes meeting his were swimming in tears. They were answer enough.

Julie knew that she and her parents could never go back to being a compact little family again, but she would be visiting them in a world which had righted itself because they were together again. She could not wait to see her grandmother's face when they returned home.

When they were on the plane with Felipe beside her holding her hand and her parents smiling at them across the gangway, Julie fell to dreaming again.

She was in the cool interior of their house in Cadiz. Felipe's ring upon her finger gleamed no less bright than the beams of sunlight creeping between the shutters on her tawny hair. She was making baby clothes. Felipe was there his dark eyes filled with love as he bent down to caress the tiny garment in her hands.

'*Mi amorada*,' he murmured, and she turned to meet the adoring eyes of her beloved.

'What are you smiling about?' he whispered.

'I'll tell you some time when we're alone,' she promised.

'It cannot come too soon for me,' he murmured, holding her small clasped hand against his tanned cheek.

'Me too,' she replied, catching her father's wink across the gangway of the plane.

A HOLIDAY HAVEN

When vacation time rolls around, most people conjure up images of golden beaches, exciting nightlife and picturesque countryside. Add to this a turquoise sea, brilliant sunshine, a taste of history and a touch of the exotic... and you come up with Majorca, the setting of *Hotel Jacarandas.*

Majorca (or Mallorca in Spanish) is the largest of the Baleares, a group of islands in the western Mediterranean, east of Spain and north of Africa. With its rich and varied culture combining Spanish and North African influences, Majorca offers the visitor a rewarding mixture of the traditional and the modern.

Most tourists arrive—by plane or boat—at the bustling port of Palma, Majorca's modern capital. Away from this glamorous center, the adventurous visitor can seek out architectural treasures and nature's wonders, such as the stunning precipitous cliffs of the north, and the spectacular stalagmite caves and subterranean lakes in the less rugged hills of the southeast. One famous island landmark for the true romantic is the abandoned monastery at Valldemosa, where famous lovers Frédéric Chopin and George Sand once lived.

Many of the island residents carry on the life-styles of their ancestors, the farmers in particular. Some of the terraces on the higher mountain slopes, where oranges, vegetables and olives grow, date back a thousand years!

Little wonder that scenic Majorca, with its ideal climate and rich heritage, is a traveler's paradise!

TAKE THESE 4 FREE

Harlequin Romances

as advertised on TV

Thrill to romantic, aristocratic Istanbul, and the tender love story of a girl who built a barrier around her emotions in ANNE HAMPSON'S "Beyond the Sweet Waters" . . . a Caribbean island is the scene setting for love and conflict in ANNE MATHER'S "The Arrogant Duke" . . . exciting, sun-drenched California is the locale for romance and deception in VIOLET WINSPEAR'S "Cap Flamingo" . . . and an island near the coast of East Africa spells drama and romance for the heroine in NERINA HILLIARD'S "Teachers Must Learn."

Harlequin Romances . . . 6 exciting novels published each month! Each month you will get to know interesting, appealing, true-to-life people . . . You'll be swept to distant lands you've dreamed of visiting . . . Intrigue, adventure, romance, and the destiny of many lives will thrill you through each Harlequin Romance novel.

Get all the latest books before they're sold out!

As a Harlequin subscriber you actually receive your personal copies of the latest Romances immediately after they come off the press, so you're sure of getting all 6 each month.

Cancel your subscription whenever you wish!

You don't have to buy any minimum number of books. Whenever you decide to stop your subscription just let us know and we'll cancel all further shipments.

Your FREE gift includes

- *Anne Hampson* — Beyond the Sweet Waters
- *Anne Mather* — The Arrogant Duke
- *Violet Winspear* — Cap Flamingo
- *Nerina Hilliard* — Teachers Must Learn

FREE GIFT CERTIFICATE

and Subscription Reservation

Mail this coupon today!

In the U.S.A.
1440 South Priest Drive
Tempe, AZ 85281

In Canada
649 Ontario Street
Stratford, Ontario N5A 6W2

Harlequin Reader Service,

Please send me my 4 Harlequin Romance novels FREE.
Also, reserve a subscription to the 6 NEW Harlequin
Romance novels published each month. Each month I will
receive 6 NEW Romance novels at the low price of $1.50
each (*Total—$9.00 a month*). There are no shipping and
handling or any other hidden charges. I may cancel this
arrangement at any time, but even if I do, these first 4 books
are still mine to keep.

_____

NAME   (PLEASE PRINT)

_____

ADDRESS

_____

CITY   STATE/PROV.   ZIP/POSTAL CODE

Offer not valid to present subscribers
Offer expires July 31, 1982   S2449